OPERATION BROADSWORD!

"Let the plan be implemented," Churchill said in a tired, almost sad, whisper.

"Broadsword?" Eden barely breathed the word.

Churchill nodded once.

"You don't actually mean to do it?"

"There's nothing else for it," said Churchill.

Only a dozen men in the entire world knew of Broadsword. Churchill realized that within a week or two, once the plan was implemented, there would be only eleven.

Or fewer. . .

TRIUMPH

BEN BOVA

TOR®

A TOM DOHERTY ASSOCIATES BOOK
NEW YORK

This is a work of fiction. All the characters and events portrayed in this book are fictitious, and any resemblance to real people or events is purely coincidental.

TRIUMPH

Copyright © 1993 by Ben Bova

All rights reserved, including the right to reproduce this book, or portions thereof, in any form.

Cover art by Tim Jacobus

A Tor Book
Published by Tom Doherty Associates, Inc.
175 Fifth Avenue
New York, N.Y. 10010

Tor® is a registered trademark of Tom Doherty Associates, Inc.

ISBN: 0-812-52063-7
Library of Congress Catalog Card Number: 92-36937

First edition: January 1993
First mass market edition: February 1994

Printed in the United States of America

0 9 8 7 6 5 4 3 2 1

To Helen and Bob Jeffries

Author's note: In the universe you and I live in, President Franklin D. Roosevelt died of a cerebral hemorrhage on 12 April 1945. Josef Stalin, dictator of the Soviet Union, lived until 1953.

1

Moscow, 1 April   How strange, thought Grigori Gagarin, to despise a man with whom I am so intimate.

He looked around the small, dark office: at the worn high-backed leather chair up on its little dais behind the plain, unpretentious desk. The desk at which the orders had been signed that coldly sent uncounted millions to their slaughter. The room was stuffy, its one window tightly sealed and curtained, confining like a prison cell, rank with the pungent burnt odor of powerful tobacco.

I hate Josef Stalin, he told himself. For the sake of my dead mother and father. For the sake of all those millions needlessly fed into the meat grinder of this endless war. For the sake of the innocents who were killed long before the war started so that Stalin could have his way, so that this upstart Georgian could rule Mother Russia with an absolute hand deadlier and stronger than any tsar's.

For the sake of my dear little brother, the only other

member of the family who still lives. But if this war goes as Stalin plans it, even little Yuri will soon enough be sucked into it and thrown to the flames, just like all the others.

Every day, all day long, ten to twelve or even sixteen hours each day, Gagarin spent within arm's reach of the man he had come to despise with a hatred as wide and deep as Mother Russia herself. Josef Stalin. The butcher. The murderer. The blunderer who had nearly lost everything to the invading Nazis.

I despise him, Gagarin said to himself for the thousandth time that morning. Then his eyes lit on the Sword hanging on the wall behind Stalin's desk. A beam of pitifully weak early April sunlight struggled through the curtains of the office's only window. It made the golden hilt of the Sword gleam.

The one door to the office swung open almost silently, but Gagarin instantly turned toward Stalin as his master, clad in an unadorned Red Army marshal's tunic and loose-fitting trousers, shuffled in, bleary-eyed and coughing. Stalin nodded perfunctorily to his private secretary, climbed the one step of the dais and settled his thick peasant's body in the worn leather chair.

Wordlessly, Gagarin moved the appointments calendar from the corner of the desk to its center. Stalin glanced at it as he reached for his pipe and the dark bowl of tobacco.

"Send in Lavrentii Pavlovich," said Stalin. His course, harsh voice grated on Gagarin's ears.

The absolute ruler of the Soviet Union had aged visibly over the past four years. The ordeal of war had grayed his hair. His once luxuriant mustache looked frayed and ragged. His face was lined and pocked like the surface of the moon. Only those in his inner circle saw him thus; to the millions beyond the Kremlin walls Stalin's image was still that of a vigorous man of middle years, the Man of Steel, the leader of Mother Russia against the invading fascists.

Wordlessly, Gagarin went to the door that opened upon the outer office. Sure enough, Lavrentii Pavlovich Beria stood at the window, gazing out at the red brick wall of the Kremlin, waiting for his master's summons like a faithful dog.

Beria's round face was pasty white. He had a high-domed forehead and thinning dark hair; a pince-nez perched on his considerable nose made his cold gray eyes seem unnervingly large. He wore his usual black funeral director's suit and tightly knotted dark tie. Every time Gagarin saw the deputy prime minister he was struck by Beria's physical resemblance to Heinrich Himmler. More than a physical resemblance: as commissar for internal affairs Beria wielded the same kind of terrifying power as the master of Hitler's SS. Even the other members of the Council of Ministers shuddered at the mere mention of his name.

Deputy prime minister of the Soviet Union and a member of the State Defense Committee, Beria had recently been named a marshal of the USSR. Gagarin saw that he was slowly gathering the reins of power into his own bloody hands. Master torturer, the secret police were already his. Patiently, relentlessly, he was worming his way into the highest levels of the Red Army through coercion, terror and betrayal.

Gagarin had seen it before. Stalin permitted one underling after another to gradually gain power. While they competed against one another they were no threat to the Man of Steel. But when Stalin sensed that one of them—any one of them, no matter who—was moving ahead of the others, that one suddenly died. He might be accused of plotting treason and sentenced to death by the courts. He might simply be thrown into one of the basement cells in Lubyanka Prison and shot in the back of the head, a sponge rubber ball stuffed in his mouth to minimize the blood spattered on the concrete floor.

But Beria troubled Gagarin. He was cold and cunning, and patient as well as ruthless. Stalin, with all the burdens of this war on his shoulders, was beginning to depend too heavily on his deputy prime minister.

"You have read Eisenhower's cablegram?" Stalin asked before Beria could even seat himself in one of the stiff wooden chairs before the desk.

Gagarin sat quietly at his own tiny desk in the far corner of the office. As Stalin's private secretary he was a fixture in the office, as unobtrusive as the silver samovar on the sideboard. I am invisible to them, he thought. Deaf, dumb and blind, as far as they care.

· Yet he was not deaf. He had heard words spoken in this office that would chill the blood of the cruelest soul. He had seen whole armies consigned to annihilation over a whim, an accident of geography, the name of a city.

"Eisenhower's cablegram?" Beria replied softly, in his whispered undertaker's voice. "The one of the twenty-eighth?" He had to look up to his master: Stalin sat on the hidden dais, and the legs of the wooden chairs had been shortened.

Stalin had puffed his pipe alight and now he waved it angrily. "Yes. What other has he sent since then?"

"He leaves Berlin to us," said Beria. Gagarin almost smiled. Lavrentii Pavlovich is waiting for his master to make his opinion clear. He is not so stupid as to take a position before he knows where Stalin's mind is.

"A transparent trick," Stalin grumbled. "An obvious attempt to lull us into inaction while the Americans and British snatch Berlin out from our grasp."

Beria stroked his soft, round chin for a moment, nodding. "Yes," he said. "I agree. A trick. Why else would Eisenhower tell us that he intends to stop his armies short of Berlin and allow us to take the city? It must be a trick."

"Of course," said Stalin.

As the two men talked—Stalin dour and suspicious, Beria smoothly accommodating—Gagarin busied his hands with the day's calendar of appointments. His head bent over the opened loose-leaf folder, his eyes stared at the page. But even as he listened to the two men across the small room, his thoughts drifted and his eyes focused on scenes from his memory.

Grigori Alekseyevich Gagarin was the elder son of a carpenter from a collective farm about a hundred kilometers southwest of Moscow. In his thirty-four years he had seen revolution and brutal civil war, the forced collectivization of farms that starved men, women and children by the millions—including his mother and father—and now this inhumanly cruel war, where hundreds of thousands of men were sent to slaughter merely by moving a pin on a map.

For the past twenty years and more he and the entire Soviet Union had been trained to adore Josef Stalin. All his school books had praised Stalin's love of knowledge and of children. A heroic statue of Stalin had been raised in the market town of Gzhatsk, where Grigori had been born, barely three months before the German bombardment destroyed it. Every radio broadcast was filled with news of Stalin. Every cinema show began with a newsreel showing Stalin bravely defending Mother Russia against the invading Nazis.

Yet Gagarin had come to hate Stalin. It was not a hot, passionate, emotional hatred boiling up from the depths of anger or jealousy. His abhorrence was coldly logical, a sharp icepick at the base of the skull, a detestation that grew more painful with every passing day, every hour.

When he had been a starveling child, watching his parents die as they gave their two sons whatever pitiful scraps of food they could glean, he had heard the whispers that Stalin was deliberately wiping out the kulaks, the independent farmers who refused to join the collectives.

When he had been in the state school for foreign service and the great purges swept thousands into their graves, he was solemnly told that all these counterrevolutionaries had been plotting to overthrow the Soviet state and its revered maximum leader, Josef Stalin. He had thought otherwise, but kept his thoughts to himself. If he spoke out, there would be no one to protect his baby brother.

A few years later, as Grigori was going through the early weeks of his first job in the great bureaucracy of the Foreign Ministry, Trotsky was hunted down in Mexico and eliminated. Everyone in the ministry professed unalloyed joy at their leader's triumph. But Grigori noticed how many trembled in their celebration. Who will be next? When will the knife turn on me?

After years of condemning Hitler and his pack of thugs, the ministry rejoiced again when Molotov signed a nonaggression pact with Nazi Germany. Rumors filtered through the ministry that the treaty included secret provisions that would allow Russia to reclaim much of the territory that the Poles had stolen and all of the Baltic states. A great diplomatic triumph engineered by the infallible Stalin.

Twenty-two months later Hitler invaded Mother Russia. Everyone was shocked to the core. Under Stalin's orders, the Soviet Union had been shipping grain and oil and metal ores to Germany by the ton, even on the very morning of the invasion. The Nazi hordes made mincemeat of the armies that Stalin insisted on directing personally. Not until Mother Russia's greatest ally of all—winter—entered the fray was the invading tide slowed and eventually stopped just short of the gates of Moscow.

Grigori had risen to Molotov's office by then. He was an efficient administrator, a rarity in the Foreign Ministry—or any other. Within a few months he was transferred to be the private secretary for Stalin himself. "The Great One has an eye for good workers," Molotov had told him personally. "I am very proud of you, Grigori Alekseyevich."

Molotov also made it clear that he expected Grigori to keep him informed of who said what to whom inside the Man of Steel's office.

It was in Stalin's office that all the old pains and doubts and terrors slowly coalesced into an icy hatred of the Great One. Grigori saw Leningrad surrounded and besieged because Stalin refused to send proper reinforcement to the "bourgeois" city. Whole armies were trapped and annihilated by the Nazi blitzkrieg because Stalin had years earlier purged most of the generals who knew anything about battle. New generals, untested except in their loyalty to the Great One who had appointed them, were summarily shot when they failed to stop the Nazi onslaught.

Gagarin's greatest fear, even greater than the terror that his hatred would somehow be discovered, was that the war would pull his little brother Yuri into its bloody jaws. Yuri was only eleven years old, but already he spoke excitedly about learning to fly and shooting the enemies of Mother Russia out of the skies.

The war is almost over, Grigori told himself time and again. The Nazis are on the brink of total defeat. But a voice inside his head would laugh derisively. The war against Germany is almost over, said the voice. Then comes the war against Japan. And after that, the war against the West. He won't stop until he is absolute master of Europe. And that means he will have to fight the Americans. There is no escaping it.

Unless someone stops him.

2

Washington, D.C., 1 April April began with a warm spring rain that brought out the Japanese cherry blossoms along the tidal basin and turned the Carrara marble of the new National Gallery a delicate rose pink. Now golden warm afternoon sunlight brightened the long windows of the Oval Office. The trill of songbirds filtered through the partially opened windows, mingled with the scent of freshly mowed grass.

Franklin Delano Roosevelt, President of the United States for the past twelve years, leaned back in his wheelchair and tried his expansive grin on his unexpected guest.

Winston Churchill scowled at his friend and comrade-in-arms. "We are not amused," he growled, "by General Eisenhower's naïveté."

"Come now, Winston," said Roosevelt, "this is no time for us to argue. The war in Europe is practically won."

"I know that. I am trying to avert the next one—against Stalin and his hordes."

Roosevelt eyed the British Prime Minister. Churchill sat before the President's desk in the Oval Office, a round little fireplug in a one-piece royal blue "siren suit," looking as defiant and pugnacious as he did in the famous portrait photograph Yousuf Karsh had made up in Canada four years earlier.

Standing somewhat uneasily by the fireplace was General George Catlett Marshall, chief of staff of the U.S. Army, tall and lean and austere. Roosevelt always thought that Marshall had the same air of incorruptible honesty and purpose that George Washington must have had. Tremendous dignity. Tremendous integrity. But cold, aloof, hardly human. Only once had Roosevelt made the mistake of calling Marshall by his first name; the general's icy stare made it clear he would tolerate no informality, not even from his Commander-in-Chief.

Only the three men were in the Oval Office. The aides that Churchill had brought with him, all the White House secretaries and staff, even the Secretary of War, Henry Stimson, had been excluded from this very private conference. No one except the President, the Prime Minister, and General Marshall.

Rummaging through the zippered pockets of his suit, Churchill broke the lengthening silence. "I must say, Franklin, that you seem to be in uncommonly good spirits."

"I feel very good. In the pink, you might say."

"You do have a healthy color to you," Churchill said, pulling his cigar case from the capacious chest pocket of his suit. "I noticed it at Yalta, in February. You appear to be in better health now than you were a year or two ago."

"I gave up cigarettes more than two years ago," Roosevelt said jauntily. "And I've never felt better."

"So that's it."

"I did it on the advice of an old acquaintance I first met during the First War, over in France in Nineteen Eighteen. A heart specialist from Boston. His name, Paul Dudley White. He warned me that if I didn't stop smoking I'd probably die of a heart attack or a stroke."

"Nonsense!" Churchill snapped. "Smoking has nothing to do with heart disease. I've been smoking all my life and look at me."

Roosevelt smiled again. "You seem rather pale and nervous, Winston."

The Prime Minister hesitated, then put the cigar carefully back into its silver case. "This Boston heart specialist hasn't talked you out of strong spirits, I hope."

Roosevelt threw his head back and laughed heartily. "No, no. Not at all. Missy will be in here with cocktails directly, I promise you."

Churchill made a tight smile back. "Good. I had feared the worst."

The President pressed a button on his intercom box, then wheeled his chair around the corner of the desk and gestured toward the pair of sofas placed on either side of the empty white marble fireplace. "Make yourself comfortable, Winston. General Marshall, you sit down, too. It hurts my neck to have to gawk up at you."

Poker-faced, Marshall folded his lanky frame into one of the sofas. Churchill took the one facing him and the President rolled his chair toward them.

The far door opened and Roosevelt's private secretary came in bearing a tray of martinis in wide-mouthed, thin-stemmed glasses. Another woman followed her with a cocktail shaker in one hand and a small bowl of olives in the other.

Once these had been set wordlessly on the low table between the sofas and the women silently had left the room, Roosevelt gestured to the cocktails, then bent forward to take one himself.

"To victory," he proposed, raising his glass.

"To clear vision," Churchill countered.

Marshall raised his glass but said nothing. He barely sipped at his martini.

"Now then, Winston, what's the trouble? What's brought you winging all the way over the Atlantic? Surely it can't be Eisenhower's memorandum."

"It most certainly is," the Prime Minister said, with some fervor. "If he's allowed to carry out the plan outlined in his memo of twenty-eighth March, it will be the biggest strategic blunder of the war."

"That plan was personally approved by the President, sir," said Marshall.

"I don't care if it was personally endorsed by Jesus Christ Almighty," Churchill snarled, "the plan is wrong. Wrong. Wrong!"

Marshall flushed and turned toward the President.

Roosevelt asked calmly, "Wrong in what way, Winston?"

"At the very least, it is the result of believing blatant Nazi propaganda," Churchill replied, pronouncing the word *Nahhzi.* "I suspect, however, far worse."

Roosevelt's cocky grin had slowly disappeared.

"I suspect that someone in Eisenhower's plans division is actively working for the Russians."

"Damn!" said Marshall, the word exploding like a pistol shot. The President looked startled: General Marshall hardly ever swore in his presence.

Pursing his lips for a moment, Roosevelt said, "Let's go down to the map room. I think we need to see the situation, not just talk about it."

"By all means," said Churchill, struggling up from the sofa.

The President led the way, rolling his chair down the West Wing corridor to the situation room he maintained on the ground floor of the main house. Churchill walked silently beside him, noting that the carpeting looked rather shabby, the walls almost seedy. *Franklin's lived here so long he's letting the place run down. Preoccupied with the business of war, just as the rest of us. No time for decorating. At least this house has not been hit by bombs, as Parliament was.*

General Marshall pulled down the big wall map of Europe while the same two women brought their drinks to the smallish room and once again closed the door behind them without uttering a word. Churchill strode to the map, peering at it as if waiting for the lines on it to move for him. The map had been updated at noon.

American and British forces were well across the Rhine and into Germany's western region. Russian army groups had overrun most of Poland and crossed the German eastern border at several points, penetrating to the River Oder.

"All right, Winston," said the President, "tell us what's on your mind."

"Berlin."

Marshall made no sound, but a nervous tic pulled at the corner of his mouth.

"The Russians are much closer to Berlin than we are," the President said, gesturing toward the map from his chair.

"We could reach it before they do, if we act vigorously," said Churchill.

The President turned to his Army chief.

"Sir," Marshall began, his voice strained, "the plan that

we have developed—and approved—calls for General Bradley's Twelfth Army Group to complete the encirclement of the Ruhr and then advance to the Elbe. Devers' Sixth Army Group is to thrust into southern Germany and Austria. Intelligence believes the die-hard Nazis are preparing a redoubt in the Bavarian Alps and we want to flush them out of there before they can fortify it strongly. Otherwise it will cost us a much higher number of casualties."

"I understand," said Roosevelt.

"What if this so-called Bavarian redoubt is a figment of Nazi propaganda?" the Prime Minister demanded.

Unflinching, Marshall replied, "So much the better. It will be less costly for us to take the territory."

"But that leaves Berlin to the Russians," Churchill muttered, still standing by the map.

"Yessir, it does," Marshall answered. "Berlin is a political symbol. My main interest is defeating the German army at the minimal cost in American lives."

"Are you implying that my interests lie elsewhere, General?"

Marshall hesitated only a moment. "Mr. Prime Minister, you are a politician. I am a soldier."

"Didn't von Clausewitz define war as an extension of politics?" Churchill asked. "Might not a soldier see that political considerations form the core of grand strategy?"

Before Marshall could reply, Roosevelt said, "Winston, there seems to be something on your mind that you haven't yet told us."

Churchill made a strange smile, almost cherubic in his fleshy face. "May I presume to offer a proposal?"

"Certainly! Certainly," the President said, wheeling over to the tray where the drinks stood.

The Prime Minister's smile turned almost puckish. Clasping his hands behind his back, he began pacing across the room on his stubby legs, speaking as he walked.

"Let us grant that there actually is a Bavarian redoubt, and it is not a work of Nazi propaganda—or Soviet misinformation."

"Granted," said Roosevelt grandly.

"Let us assume further that Hitler and his henchmen intend to repair there once their position in Berlin becomes untenable."

"Apparently Hitler has proclaimed that he will remain in Berlin, win or lose," said Marshall.

"Yes." Churchill bobbed his head. "Our intelligence people tell me the same."

"So then?" Roosevelt prodded.

Whirling back toward the map and pounding a chubby fist on the symbol marking the German capital, Churchill fairly shouted, "So rather than stopping at the Elbe, we *sweep* across the north German plain and *take* Berlin with Hitler still in it! Alive or dead, once we have him in our hands the other Nazis elsewhere will collapse and surrender."

"They wouldn't fight on?" Roosevelt asked. "They're fanatics, you know."

Churchill scowled. "You've been influenced too much by the Japanese, Franklin. The Nazi leaders are a pack of hoodlums. Once Hitler is in our grasp they'll throw down their arms and beg for mercy. You won't have to dig them out of their Bavarian redoubt, General Marshall, if it actually exists. The swine will come marching out in good order under a white flag, crying *Kamerad.*"

Roosevelt wheeled himself closer to the map. "So you think we could sweep across the open country east of the Ruhr and take Berlin before the Russians could get there? They're much closer to the city than we . . ."

"And the Germans are concentrating what forces they have left to stand between the Red Army and Berlin. There's hardly anything on the western side of the city to stop our forces, Franklin! And it's flat, open territory; good tank country. A bold, decisive thrust," Churchill said, smacking a fist into the palm of his hand, "and Berlin is ours!"

"With all due respect," Marshall said, "we tried 'a bold, decisive thrust' with Operation Market Garden last September. It bogged down at Arnhem and Montgomery never got across the Rhine."

Churchill glared at the general. "Quite frankly, I say that Berlin remains of high strategic importance. Nothing will exert a psychological effect of despair upon all German forces of resistance equal to that of the fall of Berlin. It will be the supreme signal of defeat to the German people."

"But what's the difference," Marshall countered, "if we take it or the Russians do?"

Churchill turned back to Roosevelt. "Franklin, consider: if the Russians take Berlin, will they not receive the impression that they have borne the brunt of the fighting and done the most to achieve victory? If Eisenhower's plan holds forth, Russian armies will no doubt overrun much of Austria and enter Vienna, as well. May this not lead them into a mood which will raise grave and formidable difficulties in the future?"

"Difficulties?" General Marshall asked.

The Prime Minister remained facing Roosevelt. "With the Red Army in possession of Berlin, and all the ancient capitals of Eastern Europe as well, what is to prevent them from setting up their own puppet regimes? We have already seen how they stood back while the Poles in Warsaw were exterminated by the Nazis so that they could bring in their own group of Moscow Communists to form the new Polish government. They will turn Eastern Europe into virtual colonies for themselves. Stalin will clamp the same iron dictatorship over Eastern Europe that he has over his own country. Good God! The consequences will be catastrophic. There will be no peace in Europe—Stalin's hordes will be primed to sweep westward and conquer the entire continent."

Roosevelt looked more intrigued than afraid. "Do you really think Uncle Joe would go back on the pledges he made at Yalta?"

"I have no doubt of it," Churchill said. "He already has, in Poland."

For a long moment there was utter silence in the map room.

Then Marshall said, "Our primary military objective is to defeat the German army. If we go dashing to Berlin, we could end up fighting the Russian army. The point of Eisenhower's plan is to set up clear zones and stopping points, so we don't start shooting at our allies."

"But then you let Stalin have Berlin."

"Yessir, we do. We end this war without starting another one."

Roosevelt almost sputtered into his martini. Marshall had come perilously close to accusing the Prime Minister of wanting to fight the Communists once Hitler was finished. That may be Winston's dearest heart's desire, the President told himself, but the only way it could happen would be if we do the fighting. The American people would never stand for that, he knew.

Churchill huffed and growled. The discussion went on for another hour. Seeing that General Marshall would not budge in his support of Eisenhower, and Roosevelt would not waver in his support of his chief of staff, Churchill at last excused himself and repaired to the Lincoln bedroom, where he would stay the night.

"They wouldn't buy it?" asked Anthony Eden, waiting in the upstairs hallway for his Prime Minister. Nearly a dozen aides, servants and bodyguards had accompanied Churchill on the flight across the Atlantic. Only Eden had come to the White House with him.

Tall, elegantly handsome with his graying mustache and clear blue eyes. Eden had hitched his career to Churchill's star back in those grim days when Chamberlain was trying to appease Hitler by letting him take Central Europe without firing a shot. His precisely tailored pinstripe suit made Churchill's coveralls seem rumpled and dowdy.

Churchill shook his head, his face set in a scowl of anger and impatience. "They are determined to allow Eisenhower free rein. Berlin goes to the Russians, as far as they are concerned."

"Then what are we to do?" Eden asked. Officially, he was Foreign Secretary in the British cabinet. Actually he was little more than Churchill's aide and confidant. The Prime Minister ran the foreign office personally, as he ran almost all the other departments of government.

Churchill motioned Eden into the Lincoln bedroom. Closing the heavy door carefully behind him, Eden again asked his Prime Minister, "What are we to do?"

"Let the plan be implemented," Churchill said in a tired, almost sad, whisper.

"Broadsword?" Eden barely breathed the word.

Churchill nodded once.

"You don't actually mean to do it?"

"There's nothing else for it," said Churchill.

Eden's expression hardened into a tight, bitter mask. He

left the room, closing the door so softly that it made no discernable sound.

Churchill walked past the huge, ornately carved rosewood bed and went to the window. It was April out there, warm and sunny, filled with happily chirping birds and newly blossomed flowers.

Only a dozen men in the entire world knew of Broadsword. Churchill realized that within a week or two, once the plan was implemented, there would be only eleven. Or fewer.

3

Moscow, 1 April   Grimy snow was still banked high on the streets and covered the rooftops. The sky was low and heavy with pewter-colored clouds. The setting sun barely shone through, a wan sphere without warmth. From this window, high in what had once been a royal palace, Field Marshal Georgi Zhukov noticed that there was not a tree to be seen outside the Kremlin walls. What the Nazi bombing had not destroyed in 1941 the people themselves had cut down for fuel.

He heard the door opening behind him and caught a whiff of powerful tobacco. Swiftly he whirled to stand at attention. Josef Stalin stepped into the conference room, his teeth clamped on a darkened briar pipe, his eyes glittering with secret thoughts.

Marshal Koniev, on the other side of the polished conference table, also stood at ramrod attention. Zhukov smiled inwardly. Koniev was nearly ten centimeters taller than either of them, and Stalin did not like to have men taller than himself in his presence.

"Sit, comrades," said Stalin, from behind the reeking pipe. "Sit."

Stalin wore his usual marshal's tunic, not much different from Koniev's and Zhukov's own. No medals, however, no decorations. They were not necessary for this private meeting. He sat at the head of the long table, of course. His private secretary, Gagarin, remained standing behind the generalissimo's high-backed chair. Zhukov thought of Gagarin as a ghost: silent, pale, expressionless, but always present wherever Stalin went.

The two field marshals took the chairs on Stalin's right and left, opposite one another.

"You have studied General Eisenhower's proposed plan of action?" Stalin's voice was rough as gravel, his guttural Georgian accent a pain to Russian ears.

Both field marshals nodded.

"And?"

"It fits our plans perfectly, comrade chairman," said Koniev. "The Americans and British either stop at the Elbe or head south, into Bavaria. They leave Berlin to us. And Vienna, as well."

Stalin gave him a grunt and turned to Zhukov. "And what do you have to say, comrade marshal?"

Zhukov had never trusted Koniev. The two men had been rivals since the civil war that had followed the October Revolution. Koniev had joined the Communist Party and then entered the Red Army as a Commissar. He was a brutal man, totally uncaring of the casualties he piled up as long as his troops kept moving forward. Zhukov, who had defended Leningrad, then Moscow and then Stalingrad, knew that Koniev placed his loyalty to the Party before his loyalty to the Red Army. He was ruthless, and totally subservient to Stalin.

"With the Americans and British stopping short of Berlin," Zhukov said slowly, calmly, "we can consolidate the gains we have made in the operations from the Vistula to the Oder, rest our troops, reequip . . ."

"No."

Stalin's one word halted the marshal. He glanced at Koniev, who was trying to suppress a smirk. Stalin puffed a great cloud of blue-gray smoke toward the ceiling. His eyes bored into Zhukov.

"The troops have been fighting steadily since . . ."

"No rest," Stalin said. "We will take Berlin before the Americans reach it."

"But they're not going to Berlin."

"Comrade marshal," said Stalin, "do you think I am foolish enough to believe that the Americans will allow us to take Berlin like a ripe apple hanging from a tree?"

Koniev immediately saw where his leader was heading. "Eisenhower's plan is a ruse, comrade chairman?"

Nodding vigorously, Stalin replied, "Of course it is! The Americans and British want us to believe they are not interested in Berlin. They want us to stop our advance so that they can rush across the few kilometers between them and Berlin and snatch it away from us."

Zhukov felt himself frowning. He had never been able to mask his thoughts the way Koniev could. Bradley's Twelfth Army Group was more than two hundred kilometers from the German capital, at their closest.

"Eisenhower has never lied to us, comrade chairman," he said. "The man seems touchingly open and aboveboard."

"I say he is lying," Stalin replied, in the voice that had condemned virtually all of Zhukov's old comrades in the general staff during the great purges.

Zhukov fell silent.

"Then we must move on Berlin immediately," Koniev said.

"Immediately," Stalin agreed. "But which of you will make the move?"

Zhukov quickly said, "My First Byelorussian Army Group is only eighty kilometers from the outskirts of Berlin. We have established a beachhead on the west side of the River Oder, at Kustrin. There are no further geographical obstacles between the river and the city."

Koniev countered, "My First Ukranian Army Group is poised to move at once against Berlin from the southeast. Most of the German defense units are to the east of the city, facing the Byelorussian divisions."

"But you are more than a hundred and twenty kilometers from the city," Zhukov pointed out.

"My troops are not as worn out as yours," Koniev replied sarcastically. "They do not need to rest and reequip themselves."

Zhukov felt his face flame. "My men are perfectly capable of taking Berlin! Right now!"

"The attack on the Nazi capital must be led by a man who is enthusiastic, not reluctant," Koniev shot back.

"Reluctant?" Zhukov roared. "Reluctant?"

Stalin stretched out his arms and gestured them both to silence. "I want to see your plans for taking Berlin. You have forty-eight hours to prepare them. Then I will decide which of you gets the honor."

He got up from his chair and headed for the door, Gagarin following behind him silently as a wraith. Zhukov and Koniev remained standing on opposite sides of the table, glaring at each other.

Of the many titles Josef Stalin wore, three were most important. He was Secretary General of the Central Committee of the Communist Party of the Soviet Union. He was Chairman of the Council of the People's Commissars. He was Supreme Commander-in-Chief of the Armed Forces. Thus he had consolidated in his own grasping hands the power of the Party, the government, and the army.

For all his power, his private office in the Kremlin was a small room, modestly furnished. A dark mahogany desk with a high-backed swivel chair, two straight-backed chairs in front of the desk, a sideboard with a gleaming silver samovar, and low bookcases jammed with mimeographed reports. On the walls were photographs of himself, a portrait in oils of himself, a large map of the Soviet Union pricked with tacks showing the positions of army units in three colors: black for the retreating fascists, red for loyal Soviet units, blue for Soviet groups of doubtful loyalty.

Zhukov's First Byelorussian Army Group was marked in blue. The general cared more for the army than he did for the Party, Stalin knew. Which meant that he was loyal to something other than Stalin himself. A good soldier, perhaps, but one to keep a wary eye on.

Hanging on the wall behind his desk was the Sword of Stalingrad, a gift from the English. Churchill had presented it to Stalin at the Tehran Conference, a year and a half earlier.

A two-handed Sword four feet in length, crafted in silver with a gold wire grip and a scabbard of the finest Persian lambskin, its pommel was made of clear rock crystal, marked with a gold Rose of England. The blade had been inscribed, in English on one side and Russian on the other, "To the steel-hearted citizens of Stalingrad, the gift of King George VI in token of the homage of the British people."

Stalin had accepted the bourgeois token with the idea of placing it in the War Museum, and later perhaps sending it to Stalingrad for permanent exhibit there once the war was over and the city had been rebuilt. But his private secretary had flattered him into hanging it in his private office, instead.

"After all," Gagarin had said, eyes riveted on his master rather than the English ornament, "it is you who directed the defense of Stalingrad, comrade secretary. General Zhukov and the others followed your orders. You are the one who crushed the invaders. The Sword rightfully belongs to you."

Stalin had admonished the over-eager young man. "The Sword belongs to the State, comrade."

"Oh, yes, of course. Forgive me, comrade secretary."

Smiling to show he was not angry, Stalin relented enough to say, "But perhaps it can stay in my office for a while. As a reminder to Zhukov and the other generals."

The young man had beamed his thanks.

Gagarin knew the Sword was a murder weapon. He did not know how it would accomplish its task, but he understood that it was intended to assassinate Josef Stalin.

4

Berlin, 1 April Hermann Goering was perspiring as he strode down the long concrete tunnel. Strange, he thought, to sweat when one feels the chill of death clamping down on him.

The Reichsmarschall wore his simplest uniform, the pearl gray of the Luftwaffe, knowing that Hitler detested ostentatious show from his old comrade. He'll see me sweating and think it's fear, Goering grumbled to himself. Or worse: he'll think I'm on the needle again.

Goering hated the underground bunker that the Führer had created for his headquarters. Better to be out in the open air, in the sunlight, and face the enemy man to man, he thought. But the Führer had burrowed down fifteen meters beneath Berlin's Reichstag basement, hiding out like a badger waiting to strike in the dark. Hitler had spent the whole war indoors, in the various concrete headquarters he had scattered across the greater Reich. The man did not like sunlight; strange for one who laid claim to being an artist.

Two black-uniformed SS officers led the way through the maze of tunnels, their glossy polished boots cracking like pistol shots against the bare concrete floor with each precise step. Goering tried to cheer himself with the thought that Hitler would be impressed with the weight he had lost. I'm in fighting trim, he told himself. I'm ready for anything. He dug into his tunic pocket for a handful of paracodeine pills and popped them into his mouth, chewing them furiously and swallowing them down before he reached the Führer's situation room.

He was shocked when the SS guards finally ushered him through the heavy steel door.

Adolf Hitler looked old, gray, stooped. His eyes were watery. His uniform hung limply on his shrunken frame. When he came around the big map table to greet his Reichsmarschall he shambled, lurched like a drunken man. He had to stop and grasp the edge of the map table with his left hand for support.

My god! Goering thought. He's aged ten years in the few months since I've seen him. He's a shattered man. The burdens of this war have ruined him. Then he remembered the swine who had tried to assassinate the Führer. The bomb blast must have done more physical harm than Goebbels had revealed.

"My leader!" Goering exclaimed, spreading his arms wide, marshal's baton in his left hand, as he went the final few steps toward Hitler.

"Goering," acknowledged Hitler. Nothing more. He did not even extend his hand. He kept his right hand jammed in the pocket of his gray army tunic.

There were four other men in the sunless, low-ceilinged room, and two women stenographers in army uniform. Goering recognized the hard-bitten Colonel General Gotthard Heinrici, his boots and red-striped uniform trousers spattered with mud. He must have just arrived here, Goering realized, the same as I.

The muted thud of explosions shook the bunker. Hitler looked up at the gray ceiling as dust sifted down through the shadows from the swaying overhead lights.

"The American Air Force again?" he growled.

"I don't think so," Goering replied hastily. "Russians, more likely." Luftwaffe intelligence had reported to the Reichsmarschall that the U.S. bombers had scratched Berlin from their list of targets. Now it was fair game for the Russians. Besides, Goering thought bleakly, there's hardly anything left that's worth bombing.

Hitler cast an angry scowl at Goering, with something of the old fire in his eyes. He blames me for the Luftwaffe's failure to defend our skies.

Before Goering could say anything to exonerate himself, Hitler straightened up and announced, "I asked you to come here today to witness the fact that I hereby relieve Himmler of command of Army Group Vistula. General Heinrici will assume command immediately."

Goering could not help beaming with joy. That weasel Himmler was going to get his comeuppance at last.

"I myself will personally direct the defense of Berlin," Hitler went on, his voice regaining some strength. "We will turn this city into a deathtrap for the Bolshevik barbarians. Let them come! We will slaughter them by the millions!"

Goering's joy winked off like a lightbulb shot out by a rifle bullet.

"My Führer," he said, "I agree that we can turn Berlin into a mass grave for millions of Soviet soldiers. But is it necessary for you to remain here and personally direct the battle? Would it not be safer—better for the Fatherland, that is—for you to come to Bavaria with me? My people are preparing an impregnable fortress in the mountains and—"

"Never!" Hitler snapped. He pointed at Goering with a trembling right hand. "You can go to Bavaria. I excuse you from the battle! But I will stay here to the end, whatever it may be. Victory or death! That is my destiny. That is the destiny of the German people. Victory or death."

There can be no victory, Goering said to himself. We have nothing to look forward to except death. Unless I can make a deal with the Americans and the British. That is the only way to save Germany from total annihilation.

But he kept his thoughts to himself as Hitler spent the next hour ranting against Bolsheviks in general and Stalin in particular. Finally the Führer granted Goering permission to leave. The Reichsmarschall hurried away, leaving his old comrade poring over a map and shouting instructions for moving nonexistent battalions to new defensive positions.

St. Affrique, southeastern France   Private First Class Kendall Jarvick pushed through the noisy crowd clustered around the card game and ducked out of the smoky tent, into the chill night air. He pulled a pack of Luckies from his shirt pocket, shook one loose and stuck it between his lips.

Someone flicked a Zippo lighter and held the small bluish flame to Jarvick's cigarette tip. It was Nick Hollis, the platoon's acting sergeant.

"Thanks," said Jarvick, puffing the cigarette alight.

"Tired of the game?" Hollis asked, clicking the lighter shut.

Jarvick coughed a little. Then, "I was just watching. Acey-deucey isn't my idea of fun."

"That's 'cause you never gamble. It gets more interesting when you put your money on the blanket."

"I've got better things to do with my money."

"Send it home, right?"

Jarvick nodded. The two soldiers began walking slowly down the company street: a line of big square tents set on the cold bare ground. The night sky glittered above. From somewhere in the shadows came the strains of "Moonlight Serenade" from a radio.

"I still feel bad about Glenn Miller," Jarvick said, trying to shift the subject.

"Yeah, that was a shame. But his orchestra's still going strong."

Just like us, thought Jarvick. No matter how many men get killed or wounded, no matter who leaves the outfit for whatever reason, the outfit goes on: squad, platoon, company, battalion, regiment, division—the whole blasted Army, it just goes on and on, no matter what.

Hollis knew Jarvick's silences. Jarvick was the platoon's intellectual, a guy who had been to college and worked as a newspaper writer before the war. Nick Hollis believed that after the fighting was all finished Jarvick would go back to Iowa and write a book about the war, about their unit: the 101st Airborne. Maybe he'll write something about me, Hollis thought. That'd be funny.

I wonder how I look to him? The two soldiers had been in the same squad for more than a year now; never close enough to be real buddies, but they had looked out for each other in combat. Then Hollis shrugged to himself. Hell, you look out for everybody in the friggin' squad when you're in combat. You got to. Otherwise nobody lasts long.

Jarvick puffed silently on his cigarette, thinking that the unit's long rest since Bastogne must be really working. A few weeks ago, if somebody had come up behind me in the dark and suddenly flipped on his lighter I would've jumped out of my skin.

"How long do you think it's gonna last?" Hollis asked.

"Huh?"

"The war. How much longer do you think it's gonna go on?"

Jarvick shook his head. "I don't know. Can't be much longer. Hitler's beaten, he's just not admitting it."

"Yeah."

They walked to the end of the dirt street. It had not rained in days so the ground was firm and dry. Good weather for tanks, Jarvick thought.

"You gonna go back to your newspaper job after the war?" Hollis asked as they turned around and started back toward their own tent.

Jarvick nodded, then realized that Hollis probably couldn't see the gesture in the starlit darkness.

"Yes," he said.

"You're married, right?"

"Yes."

"Any kids?"

"No. Not yet."

Jarvick knew it was a mistake to get too close to anyone. You shouldn't make friends of men who might get themselves killed a week or a month from now. It was too painful. Despite himself he had become almost fatherly to that big lunkhead Sturgis from Kentucky and the poor hillbilly got it at Bastogne. Jarvick still thought about the big kid with his lopsided grin and that everlasting twang in his voice.

"What did you do before the war?" he asked Hollis, more to get his mind off Sturgis than any other reason.

"Me? This and that. I never had much of a steady job."

"Really?"

"I did a lot of traveling. On the road almost all the time. Worked when I had to. Chased women, mostly. I was havin' a lot of fun until Uncle Sam caught up with me."

Jarvick almost smiled. "Nick, you sound like a grasshopper."

"Me?"

"You know the old story about the grasshopper and the ant?"

"Oh, yeah." Hollis laughed aloud. "I guess you're right. That's me, all right. Until I found a home in the Army."

They were back at their own tent. They could see the silhouettes of the men crouching around the blanket they had spread on the ground, crowding around their card game; their raucous voices almost drowned out the radio's "String of Pearls."

Jarvick did not want to go back inside. It was shivering cold out here, but he could not bring himself to go back into the smoke-filled tent while the card game was still going on.

"What are your plans for after the war?" he asked Hollis.

In the light leaking from the tent, Hollis' face looked almost startled. "After the war? I don't know. Haven't given it much thought. Guess I'll look around for a while. There's still a lot of the States I haven't seen yet."

Jarvick muttered, "Uh-huh."

"You're going back to Iowa, you said."

"Right. Back to Turnersville. Back where I belong."

"Lived there all your life?"

Jarvick nodded. "Except for college."

Hollis grinned at him. "Well, if I'm a grasshopper, you're sure an ant."

Jarvick grinned back. "I guess I am. I guess I'm happy to be."

"Yeah. If you can do what you like to do, that's when you're happy."

The cigarette was down to a butt barely a finger's width long. Jarvick flipped it into the shadows between tents.

"Yep. All we've got to do is live through the next few weeks and we can go home."

"You think it'll be over in a few weeks? That soon?"

"It's got to be," Jarvick said. "The Germans can't have much left to fight with."

Hollis cocked his head slightly to one side, as if deep in thought. Then he said, "I just hope that the Army can get the job done without needing us in the line again."

"That would be fine by me," Jarvick agreed. "I've seen enough of this war."

"Amen, brother!"

The two men stood uncertainly in front of the tent. They had nothing more to say to one another. Jarvick shifted uneasily. Hollis stamped his booted feet against the night cold.

"I think I'll go in and get into the game," Hollis said at last. "There oughtta be enough money on the blanket to make it interesting by now."

"Why don't you clean them all out in a hurry so I can get some sleep?"

"I'll try."

"Good luck."

"Yeah. Thanks."

Hollis ducked through the tent flap, to be greeted by hoots of derision when he announced he had come to show them how the game should be played.

Jarvick stayed outside, smoked another cigarette and then another, arms hugging himself for warmth, feeling as alone as a Martian in a strange alien world.

5

Washington, D.C., 1 April   Franklin Roosevelt sat in his wheelchair, alone in the White House map room, studying the disposition of the troops across Europe. Churchill had departed for London, still grumbling that the Allies could and should take Berlin.

"The Germans will fight to the last man against the Russians," Churchill had warned. "They are frightened to death of the Bolsheviks, and they have good cause to fear vengeance, after the havoc they have wreaked in the Soviet Union. But they will surrender willingly to the British and Americans, Franklin. They will be happy to lay down their arms to our troops."

Perhaps so, Roosevelt thought as he stared at the big wall map. But the Germans fought hard, very hard—until we crossed the Rhine. Now they seem to be disorganized, discouraged.

"Franklin, are you ever coming to dinner?"

He turned his head and saw his wife standing in the doorway, with that slightly pained look that she so often wore.

"In a moment, Eleanor," he said.

She entered the map room and sat on the chair nearest her husband. "You've been moody ever since Winston left. What's the problem?"

Eleanor was far from beautiful; newspaper cartoonists exaggerated her large teeth and homely features almost as often as they lampooned Roosevelt's own jaunty grin and long cigarette holder—even though he had not touched a cigarette for more than two years now. Her voice was high and thin and trembling; she had sounded like an old woman when she had been a skinny, spindly teenager. Franklin had not always been faithful to her and she knew it.

Yet she stayed at his side, a proud woman of high intelligence and higher purpose. More than anyone except his dear departed Mama, Eleanor had recognized the greatness in Franklin and had worked tirelessly to help him achieve his destiny. When polio struck and crippled his legs and he wanted nothing more than to die, it was Eleanor who kindled the fire of resistance in him. Night and day she encouraged, pleaded, cajoled, fought to make him realize that his life was not over, that his political ambitions depended on nothing more than his own will to conquer his handicap.

She succeeded, and then he succeeded. Once he became President, Eleanor became his eyes and ears, traveling where he could not easily go, listening to voices that would have been too shy or frightened or perplexed to speak to the President of the United States himself.

"Are you all right, Franklin? You look tired."

He said nothing.

"What's the problem?" she asked again, more softly.

Roosevelt wheeled his chair around to face her, putting his back to the map.

"Berlin," he said, suddenly weary, spent, exhausted by the years of decisions that sent young men to their graves.

Eleanor guessed, "Winston wants us to take it?"

"It would mean a great deal more casualties."

"Would it mean anything more than that?"

Wishing he had a cigarette, Roosevelt answered, "Of course it would. If we take Berlin, instead of the Russians doing it, we'll be in a much better position after the shooting stops."

"A better position against whom, Franklin?"

"Uncle Joe and his Bolsheviks, who else?"

"But I thought," Eleanor said, "that you got along well with Stalin. You told me you could handle him."

Roosevelt gave her a glum look. "I may have been exaggerating my powers of persuasion, Eleanor dear. The Communists have taken over Poland and won't allow free elections. I fear they'll be doing that in all the countries they've liberated from the Nazis—Romania, Bulgaria, Hungary. Even Czechoslovakia and Austria, if we allow them to."

"If we allow them to," Eleanor echoed. Her voice sounded firm and final, despite its tremulous falsetto.

"It will kill thousands upon thousands of American boys to take Berlin. We could end up fighting each other, the Russians and us. That's what bothers me most; the thought of our troops and the Russians fighting each other."

"There are the Japanese to consider, too," Eleanor said. "We'll still have that war to fight even after Hitler is finished."

He gave a cheerless nod. "Yes. They fought to the last man on Iwo Jima and now they're sending suicide planes against our fleet at Okinawa. It's going to be the worst bloodbath of them all when we invade their home islands."

"So you want to save as many lives in Europe as possible."

"Of course. We're going to need those troops."

"Then let Berlin go, if it's not worth the price."

"That's just it," Roosevelt said, his temples throbbing. "I'm not sure if it's worth the price or not. It would be horrible if we beat Hitler to free the people of Europe, only to find that Stalin takes them into his grip."

Eleanor got to her feet and walked around behind his wheelchair. She started pushing him toward the corridor and the elevator that would take them up to their family quarters and dinner.

"Franklin, you've had the responsibility for many, many difficult decisions for more than twelve years now. I'm certain that you will make the best decision about this. You always do."

He shook his head, wishing that he had as much confidence in himself as she did.

That night, as he sat alone in his bed with an unopened report on his lap, Roosevelt tried to picture what Europe would look like once the fighting ended. Germany devastated. Cities bombed and shelled into rubble. Farmlands torn up by the treads of tanks, forests shattered, livestock slaughtered. The rest of Europe much the same: France, Italy, the countries to the east where the Red Army had thundered through. No factories left standing. No food. No coal for heat in the winter.

According to the plans made at Yalta the Soviets would control half of Germany and Austria and all the nations of Eastern Europe. Stalin had promised to allow free elections but Roosevelt knew how promises can be evaded, postponed, negated by the tide of events.

Winston fears that Uncle Joe will turn Eastern Europe into a Soviet colony. He's already setting up his own puppet government in Poland. And there are huge Communist parties in Italy and even in France; what's to stop Stalin from moving on them?

But a countering thought nagged at him. For all Winston's dedication to democracy, the man's highest loyalty is still to the British Empire. He wants to preserve British influence in the Middle East; he wants to maintain Britain's control of India. Winston sees the Russians much as Rudyard Kipling saw them: "Beware the bear that walks like a man."

Roosevelt realized that Churchill had fought for the British Empire as a cavalry officer while Kipling was still writing about "the white man's burden." He almost smiled, there in his bed.

But his thoughts sobered him. *I must be careful not to allow Winston to draw America into conflict with the Russians merely to save what's left of the British Empire. It's one thing to work for the freedom of the Europeans whom Hitler enslaved. It's quite another thing to work for the salvation of Winston's beloved Empire. I've got to be very careful about this. Very careful indeed.*

But if Uncle Joe really does intend to turn Eastern Europe into a Soviet colony, it will mean war, Roosevelt realized. *Sooner or later we'll have to draw a line and try to stop them. The British don't have the strength to do it; their fight against Hitler has drained them dry. There's no one else except us. Us against the Russians.*

What can I do? Roosevelt asked himself. *What can I do to save us from this awful predicament?* For one of the rare moments in his life Roosevelt felt helpless, lost and alone. Eleanor was in her own room. The entire household was asleep. His wheelchair stood empty and worn beside the bed, within arm's reach. He looked down at his crippled legs so frail and thin beneath the bedsheet and wished desperately that there was some way out of the dismal vortex that he foresaw.

Berlin. If we did take Berlin, would that discourage Stalin from his plans of expansion? Would it show Uncle Joe that we don't intend to allow him a free hand in Eastern Europe? Or will it just start us shooting at one another all the sooner?

In politics, he reminded himself, you seldom have the luxury of a clear-cut choice. You always have to be satisfied with the lesser of two evils.

He reached for the telephone and dialed General Marshall's home number.

The phone rang once, then the general's crisp voice said, "Marshall here." As if he had been sitting by the phone all evening, waiting for this call.

"General," said Roosevelt, his tone instantly brightening when he had an audience other than Eleanor, "I'm sorry to disturb you at this time of night."

"Mr. President," came Marshall's voice through the phone, tight with expectation.

"General, your plans people have a contingency plan drawn up for Berlin, don't they?"

A moment's hesitation. Then, "Yes, sir, we do. It hasn't been updated for several months, however."

"Well, could you brush it up and let me see it tomorrow or the day after?"

"Yes, sir, Mr. President. Um—Mr. Stimson should participate in any decisions along this line."

Henry Stimson, the Secretary of War, would back Marshall to the hilt, Roosevelt knew. Neither of them felt that Berlin was worth the candle.

"Oh, I don't intend to change any of the decisions we've

already made," Roosevelt temporized. "I just want to see how we might go about it—if there should be some reason to. If the situation should suddenly change."

"I see," said General Marshall.

"Thank you, General. I'll call Henry now.'

Above the Atlantic, 2 April The ponderous flying boat was noisier than a herd of trumpeting elephants and vibrated like a palsied old man. Yet Churchill had slept well in the bunk that had been fitted up for him in the rear cabin, dreaming of friends long since departed. He awoke early enough, though, to watch the dawn breaking through the clouds.

A symbol, perhaps, he thought as he pulled on his silk robe and tied its sash around his portly middle. The aroma of frying bacon and perking coffee wafted into his cubicle. That was one thing about the Americans: they never let you go home hungry. The Yanks complained about food rationing, but their daily allotment of meat and milk was more than the average Briton got in a month.

Stepping through the curtain that screened off his cubicle, Churchill saw that his valet had already prepared his morning whiskey and water. The shaving things were waiting by the porthole, where the sunlight glinted off the steel-gray water below. Across the vibrating aluminum flooring, two Royal Navy ratings were setting a folding table with a white tablecloth and dishes for two.

A full squadron of P–38 Lightnings had escorted the flying boat from Washington to the full limit of their range. Spitfires would greet the plane later in the day, as it approached the home islands. For now, over the middle of the wide ocean, the Sunderland flew alone.

If only the Luftwaffe knew, Churchill said to himself, a grim smile curling his lips. How happy Hitler would be to shoot me down. Of course, his own fighters do not have the range to reach this far over the ocean. But he has those blasted Fock-Wulf bombers still sneaking around out here. What do they call them? The Condor. Yes, that's their name for the plane. Condor. The Nazis love names like that. Vultures and Tigers and such. The Eagle's Nest. What is it Hitler calls his headquarters? The Wolf's Lair. The hyena's den, more likely.

Eden ducked through the hatch that led up to the cockpit, natty as ever in a gray three-piece suit, and saw the breakfast table being prepared by the two seamen. Churchill accepted his morning whiskey from his valet and gestured grandly toward the table.

As he and Eden sat on the rickety folding chairs, Churchill asked over the bellowing of the plane's engines, "What news?"

"Nothing that can't wait until after breakfast," Eden replied. He looked tense, though.

"Broadsword?"

Eden lowered his voice until it could barely be heard over the roar of the engines. "The order went out last night, as you instructed. We received an acknowledgment from the embassy in Moscow with this morning's radio dispatches."

"Then the plan is in motion."

"Yes, it is."

Churchill ran a hand across his stubbly jaw. "Now it all depends on some Russian we've never seen."

"It's a shaky scheme, at best, Winston. If Stalin finds out about it, or even his successors, should it be successful . . ."

"There's nothing to suggest that we did it," Churchill said. "They will suspect traitors in their own midst. That's the Russian way."

"They don't have plutonium," Eden pointed out.

"Then they won't know what it is, will they?"

Eden puffed out a nervous sigh. "I must say, Winston, that you seem quite calm about the whole thing."

Churchill allowed one of the sailors to serve him a large plate of bacon and scrambled eggs while he sipped at his whiskey. The empty tea cups rattled on their saucers like nervous old women.

"There is only one point that worries me," he said after the man had left their table.

"What is that?"

"Will he do it? Will the Russian chap that our embassy people have picked out actually have the nerve to do the job?"

6

Berne, 2 April   Clouds of thick gray smoke wafted silently to the high rococo ceiling of the luxurious Swiss hotel room as Allen Dulles puffed reflectively on his pipe. It was the tactic he used when he was unsure of himself, faced with a problem or a person he could not fathom. Smoke signals to nowhere.

Sitting on the oversized wingback chair before him was General Karl Wolff, his bald, round face bearing a small but noticeable dueling scar on his left cheek. Chunky build. In a three-piece tweed suit of light brown, his legs crossed, a cigarette pointing straight up in the air between his two fingers and thumb, General Wolff looked relaxed, at ease, almost like a vacationing tourist instead of the commander of the SS in Italy.

Dulles studied Wolff for long moments as he puffed on his pipe. Head of the U.S. Office of Strategic Services in Europe, Dulles looked more like a schoolmaster than a master spy. He too wore a tweed jacket, dark blue, with leather patches on the elbows. His gabardine trousers were darker, navy blue, and he wore a sleeveless vee-neck gray sweater in place of a vest.

"Let me see if I understand you correctly," said Dulles. His voice was thin, soft.

"It is very simple," General Wolff replied crisply. "General Kesselring will agree to an immediate armistice for all the German forces under his command. That includes the entire Italian theater."

"What's left of it," Dulles murmured.

Wolff's light gray eyes flashed, but he went on as if he had not heard the comment. "All German forces will withdraw in good order with their field equipment, food, fuel and ammunition. As part of the agreement we pledge not to fight against the British or American forces still in the field. You will gain all of Italy, right up to the border of Austria, without firing another shot or incurring another casualty."

Dulles took the pipe from his lips. "And General Kesselring can march his troops to your eastern front to fight the Russians."

"Precisely so."

"But the Russians are our allies."

Wolff forced a smile. "Come now, sir. A pack of barbarians raping and looting their way across Eastern Europe? Your allies?"

Dulles thought about the way the SS had treated the Russians and Ukrainians and all the others that had fallen into their clutches. The death camps. The slave labor. The extermination of what Hitler called *untermensch* to give the true Aryan Germans *lebensraum,* room to live in.

He asked, "What does Berlin have to say about General Kesselring's proposal?"

Wolff's smile tightened.

"Does Hitler approve of giving up what you still hold in Italy?"

Through clenched teeth, Wolff said, "That is none of your affair. General Kesselring has made a most generous offer. What is your response?"

Dulles looked down at his pipe, saw that it had gone out. He got to his feet and walked across the carpeted floor to the desk. A wonderful prop, he thought. That's what a pipe is. Gives you an excuse for not answering immediately. Gives you time to think. Makes you look wise.

He rapped the pipe sharply on the heavy porcelain ashtray on the desk, knocking out the blackened dottle of ash on the first shot. Let him stew a few moments, Dulles thought to himself. I'm in no hurry. He fished in his jacket pocket for the pouch of tobacco he had brought with him. Turning back toward the German and half-sitting on the desk as he dug the pipe into the sweet-smelling blend, he said at last:

"I can't believe that General Kesselring is acting on his own in this. If this is part of a larger deal that Hitler wants to make, I need to know about it now. However, if General Kesselring *is* doing this on his own volition, how does he expect to withdraw his troops from Italy against Hitler's express orders to stand and fight? We know what's happened to other generals who tried to go against Hitler's will. Even Rommel." Tamping the tobacco in the pipe's bowl with his thumb, Dulles added, "At least your SS didn't hang him with piano wire, like some of the others."

Wolff's smile returned, but this time his eyes glittered with a barely repressed anger.

"My dear Mr. Dulles," he said, slowly, choosing his words carefully, "I have never before heard of a man refusing to accept the withdrawal of an entire army. I assure you, General Kesselring can and will pull his troops peacefully from Italy and will never use them against British or American forces."

"Never?"

"Never. Our Fatherland has been invaded by howling barbarian hordes from the east. The very life of Germany is at stake. In all honesty, we need every man and weapon we possess to defend ourselves against the Bolshevik monsters. This has nothing to do with politics. If they—"

Dulles stopped him with an upraised finger. Crossing the room swiftly to sit before the SS general once more, he asked, "Are you saying that *all* the German forces facing us are willing to surrender?"

Wolff stubbed his cigarette on the ashtray standing next to his chair. It was time for him to think carefully before answering.

"I would not use the word 'surrender.' "

"An armistice, then?" Dulles asked. "All the German forces in Italy *and* the western front?"

"I am not empowered to discuss that." Before Dulles could respond, Wolff went on, "However, General Kesselring is very influential among the other field commanders."

Dulles shook his head. "No, there's more to it than Kesselring. Who's behind this? What's really going on?"

Wolff leaned back in his chair and took a silver cigarette case from his inside jacket pocket. "As I have said, General Kesselring is very influential. He has many friends and comrades in positions of high command."

Hunching forward, his pipe still unlit in his hand, Dulles mused aloud, "Kesselring is certainly one of the most respected field commanders from our point of view. And he was a Luftwaffe general, too, wasn't he? Earlier in the war he . . ."

Dulles stopped. His brown eyes widened.

"Goering! Kesselring is acting as a stalking horse for Goering!"

Wolff said nothing.

"Goering's behind this, isn't he?" Dulles demanded. "He's willing to make an armistice with the Anglo-American forces so that he can shift all the German power to the east, against the Reds!"

Silently, Wolff lit his fresh cigarette. Then he calmly asked, "Would you like to meet the Reichsmarschall?"

"Here?"

"No, no." With a shake of the head, *"Der Dicke* is far too well known to leave Germany without being observed. He has a castle in Bavaria, however. Near Nuremberg. I could arrange for you to meet with him there."

Dulles sank back in his chair, mind spinning. Hermann Goering: the number two man in Germany. Highest ranking military officer in the Third Reich. His star has sunk pretty low, true enough. But he's still legally Hitler's heir and successor. He stuck his dead pipe in his teeth and steepled his fingers before his face, thinking furiously.

The generals had tried to assassinate Hitler the previous July. It didn't work and anyone vaguely suspected of being in on the plot had been executed, horribly. At least they allowed Rommel to take poison.

Is Goering trying to take over? Push Hitler aside or even assassinate him, in the name of saving Germany from the Russians? Dulles had to work hard to keep his face from betraying his hopes.

"Our policy is unconditional surrender," he said at last to Wolff. "You know that. And we could never accept a surrender that does not include our Russian ally."

"We know your policy very well," Wolff replied stiffly. "It is quite unworkable, given the actual military and political situation. I believe that the Reichsmarschall has a plan that will save many British and American lives."

"And what about Hitler?"

"That is neither your concern nor mine. Are you willing to meet with the Reichsmarschall or not?"

"I'll have to get in touch with Washington. I can't do this without higher approval."

"I understand."

Dulles ushered the SS general to the door of his hotel suite. Two tall husky blond men in ill-fitting civilian suits stood waiting outside in the corridor, trying their best to look inconspicuous.

Goering! Dulles thought as he closed the door after bidding Wolff good-bye. We could end the war in a few days, maybe. At least, our part of it.

He practically pranced to the telephone and ordered a car to take him to the U.S. embassy.

London, 2 April   "Why do you ask?"

Fuchs said it mildly, casually, hiding the sudden stab of fear that his friend's question had stirred in him.

Powys gave one of his elaborate Welsh shrugs, which involved his shoulders, arms, hands, eyebrows, even his expressive lower lip. "Curiosity, actually. It's rather frustrating being a courier without knowing much about the stuff one's carrying back and forth."

The two men were sitting in leather armchairs in the reading room of Powys' club, leaning close to one another, speaking in the hushed tones that the club rules demanded. They would have been whispering wherever they were, for they were talking about a subject that bore the security classification of TOPMOST SECRET: NEED TO KNOW ONLY.

Klaus Fuchs was a spare man, with graying hair fast receding from his bulbous forehead. Thick rimless eyeglasses made him appear to be squinting all the time. Before the war a man would have dressed in dinner clothes to come to the club at this time of the evening. But Fuchs was in a rumpled suit that had seen much wear. He seemed awkwardly out of place in the club, unable to relax, a foreigner, a refugee. He was also a scientist. And a spy.

Powys was a huge contrast. He looked exactly like what he was, a salty old sea dog: barrel-chested, heavy-armed, big broad face with shaggy brows and an unruly mane going gray but still thick as a mop. He was in mufti, an ancient blue serge suit that fitted him poorly and tended to shine at the knees and elbows. His rugged face was deeply tanned, but he had spent more time in the desert these past two years than at sea.

He also happened to be a viscount whose great-great-grandfather had founded this particular gentleman's club.

"Plutonium," Fuchs muttered, breathing the word so softly that Powys had to lean forward in his chair to hear the man.

"That's the stuff. What is it, exactly? The Yanks in New Mexico wouldn't tell me a word. Not even our own chaps would say much, except that it's devilishly dangerous."

"It is very dangerous."

"Some kind of poison, then?" Powys asked, leaning even closer to Fuchs.

"This is very hush-hush, you realize." Fuchs seemed uncomfortable, squirming in his chair as if there were other things living in his clothes along with him.

"I understand that."

"You say they asked you to carry some plutonium here from New Mexico?"

Powys nodded eagerly. "Yes. Two years ago."

"Two years ago?"

"I recall it had something to do with the conference in Tehran. Or so I got the feeling at the time. No one actually told me so, of course."

"Of course." Fuchs leaned back in his chair, steepling his fingers. They had downed two sherries each before Powys had asked his question. Staring worriedly at his companion, Fuchs told himself, It cannot be more than curiosity, just as he says. He had only known Powys since he had been assigned to be liaison between the British nuclear program and the Americans' Manhattan Project. Still, he could not believe this big, blunt errand boy could be a counter-espionage agent.

Yet, one cannot be too careful, Fuchs reminded himself. If he *is* working for MI5 . . .

"How dangerous a poison is it?" Powys asked, his brow furrowed.

Fuchs made a quick decision. I will tell him as much as a good friend would tell. Nothing more.

"If you have not been exposed to it in two years, you have nothing to worry about. It did not harm you, apparently."

"I wasn't worried about that. I'm just damned curious why it's all so hush-hush. I can understand that this business of making a super-bomb should be kept quiet. But how did they get into the business of making poison? We're not going to use poison gas, are we? That would be a violation of the Geneva Convention, wouldn't it?"

Fuchs forced himself to smile. "It has nothing to do with poison gas. Plutonium is a new element, rather like radium. It is dangerous because it gives off harmful radiation. It must be sealed in lead or else the radiation could be deadly."

"Oh. I see."

"Do they want you to carry more of it?" Fuchs asked, wondering where this trail might lead.

Powys shook his massive head, making his mop of hair flop over his shaggy brows. "No, not at all."

Two years ago, Fuchs thought.

"Odd thing, though," said Powys. "If it must be kept behind lead, as you say, then I couldn't have been carrying more than half an ounce of the stuff. The box they gave me couldn't have weighed more than a pound. It fit inside my dispatch case quite easily."

"It all happened two years ago, you say?"

"Eighteen months, two years—somewhere around then."

"About the time of the Tehran Conference?"

"Just before then," said Powys. "I remember wondering if it had anything to do with the conference. I suppose not, actually."

"If I were you," Fuchs said, steepling his fingers again, "I would forget about the entire matter. And for heaven's sake, do not ask anyone else about it. It is an extremely sensitive subject."

"Yes, I see," said Powys, his brow knitting even harder. He understood that something very deep and dark was involved here, and although he was still extremely curious he knew better than to press the matter further.

They spoke of other matters during dinner. Fuchs noted that despite wartime rationing the club members ate quite well. Typical of the English, he thought. The whole nation is locked in a death struggle with the Nazis, but the upper class makes fewer sacrifices than the working masses. And they think nothing of it. As if it is their due.

The only reason he invited me here tonight was to pump me about the plutonium. Could he truly have waited two years to worry over it? Fuchs realized he would have to be extraordinarily careful. Powys might be no more than an upper-class errand boy, but he might be doing errands for MI5 now, instead of the nuclear bomb project.

Still—this was a tantalizingly important piece of information. The Americans sent a sample of plutonium to their British cousins nearly two years ago. It must have been some of the very first plutonium they managed to refine. Two years ago. Just before the Tehran Conference.

No matter what the risks, Fuchs decided that Moscow must be told of this. Immediately.

7

Moscow, 2 April   Grigori Gagarin had actually set up a tape recorder in the bedroom of his apartment more than two years earlier. It had been fairly difficult to get one; such machines were not handed out willingly by the Kremlin's quartermaster office. But the private secretary to Chairman Stalin encountered less trouble than most.

Gagarin needed to know if he talked in his sleep. If Beria became suspicious and planted a microphone in his bedroom, what would he hear? For weeks Gagarin spent an hour or so before bedtime listening to the previous night's tape, leaning bleary-eyed over the big cumbersome box while the spools slowly turned, trying to make some sense out of the snores and grunts that he heard.

He wished he could have requisitioned a voice-activated machine. He had heard Beria describe one to Stalin once: the machine turned itself on automatically when there were sounds to record; otherwise it stayed off. That would have made it easier than poring over hours of taped silence.

Still, silence was good. Silence was safe. After many months Gagarin stopped listening to himself, put the tape machine in a closet and tried to forget about it. Then Yuri came home for the year's-end vacation from school and discovered it. Fascinated with gadgets of any type, Yuri played for hours with the tape machine. It chilled Gagarin's blood every time he saw his little brother with it.

But something else had frightened Gagarin even more.

"I'm going to start taking flying lessons!" Yuri had excitedly announced as soon as he saw his older brother, at the train station.

"Nonsense," Grigori had snapped. "You're much too young."

As they worked their way through the crowd at the train platform, Yuri clutching his little lunchbox and Grigori with his brother's suitcase firmly in his grip, Yuri explained that the school was allowing the very best students to take preliminary flying lessons—on the ground, in a classroom only.

Relieved, Grigori said, "Then you won't actually be flying."

"Not this year. But if I do well in my studies next year they'll take me up in a plane. And when I'm fourteen I can join the Air Pioneers!"

The busy railroad station seemed to disappear from Grigori's awareness. The noisy, shouting crowd, the hissing, chuffing locomotives, the booming announcements echoing from the loudspeakers, even the heat and the smell of too many sweaty bodies pressing too closely together—all that faded from his consciousness. All that Grigori could see was his baby brother in a military uniform, eyes closed, hands folded peacefully over his breast, lying in a rough wooden coffin.

"I don't want you to go flying," he said testily. "It's dangerous."

Yuri laughed a youthful innocent laugh. "Every student has to join one of the Pioneer groups. I chose flying. They only allow the students with the best grades to get into the Air Pioneers."

The youngster was proud of his achievement and eager to test his wings. With a sinking heart Grigori realized that if Yuri was blocked from the path that led to flying he would end up in the infantry or the tank corps. Every boy his age was going to be a warrior, one way or the other. As long as Stalin pursued his dreams of conquest.

Gagarin's descent into treason had started innocently enough. Like many Russian tragedies, it had begun with a drinking bout.

More than two years earlier, when Churchill and his entourage had visited Moscow the first time, Gagarin found himself assigned to entertain four of the lesser Englishmen while Stalin and the British Prime Minister closeted themselves in the Great One's office with Molotov and a pair of interpreters. Stalin always kept late hours, and apparently Churchill did too. The two of them met at ten in the evening to begin their dinner and discussions. Rarely did they stop before dawn.

Gagarin's task was a delicate one. He had to keep the quartet of British underlings reasonably happy and available to answer any questions that their master might bring up all through the long night and early morning. He also had to make certain that the capitalists had no opportunity to see or hear or even sniff anything that they should not know. A visiting diplomat was a visiting spy, as far as Stalin was concerned.

So Gagarin set up one of the small meeting rooms near Stalin's office as an impromptu dining hall and had dinner brought in. He invited two young women to join them; one of them, from the typing pool, was lovely enough to have aroused Gagarin's own interest. The other posed as a typist but was actually from Beria's MGB, the Ministry for State Security.

Two of the Englishmen were interpreters, so they spoke Russian. Although Gagarin could read English, he doubted his ability to pronounce it well and to think quickly enough to hold a conversation. Besides, it would draw suspicion on himself to speak to foreigners in their own tongue.

There were many toasts during their dinner, much laughter and pledging of solidarity against the Nazis and eternal friendship. Hours passed, and although the food was long demolished into crumbs and stains on the tablecloth, the vodka was constantly renewed by a pair of unsmiling waiters in black suits. Also MGB, Gagarin knew.

"Bloody shame you people didn't trust us," said one of the Englishmen, drunk enough to lapse into his native tongue. He was rail-thin, with a cadaverous pasty white face and dark sunken cheeks. Straw-colored hair had pasted itself sweatily over his brow and he constantly pawed at it ineffectually.

"I beg your pardon," Gagarin said in Russian. He felt pleasantly buzzed. The evening had been a happy success. The Englishmen were easy enough to get along with and the vodka has loosened most of Gagarin's tensions. Best of all, the young typist was smiling at him warmly.

"Oh, don't mind Sandy," said one of the others. "He's in his cups. He always gets very serious when he's had too much to drink."

"I said it was a terrible shame," Sandy spoke in slurred Russian, "that you didn't trust us back in Forty-one when we tried to warn you about Hitler's attacking you."

Gagarin glanced at the secret policewoman. She was allowing one of the Englishmen to nuzzle her ear, but her eyes were locked on Sandy.

"We received no warning," said Gagarin. "The Nazi attack was a complete surprise to us. A typical piece of Hitlerite deceit."

"Well, we certainly tried to warn you," Sandy insisted. "Two months before the invasion began, at least. I should know. I coded the cablegram that Winston sent to our ambassador in Moscow."

"Come on Sanders old chap," said the man to his right. He seemed more sober than the others. Probably their secret police agent. "Don't be so melancholy. It's all water under the bridge now. Ancient history."

"Uhmm," Sandy murmured. "Still, you could have saved millions of lives if you had listened to us. We told you the truth but you wouldn't believe us."

He said it in English. Gagarin felt a trembling panic in his stomach. Should I ask him to repeat what he has said in Russian or just ignore the whole thing?

"Another toast!" said the pretty one from the typing pool. "To friendship and happiness."

"Hear, hear!" said all the Englishmen as one.

The long night ended and the Englishmen were taken back to the hotel that had been provided for them. Gagarin never spoke another word to Sandy, whoever or whatever he was. But he wondered for months if the man had spoken the truth. Had the English warned Stalin that Hitler was going to attack Mother Russia? Did Stalin ignore the warning out of blind stupidity or for some hidden reason of his own? Whole armies had been destroyed in that first furious

Nazi onslaught. Two-thirds of the European part of the Soviet Union had fallen to the invaders. Millions of women and children were still under the jackboots of Hitler's Gestapo and SS.

Gagarin could not believe Stalin had blundered. If he knew that the Nazis were going to attack and did nothing to prepare the nation for the ordeal there must have been some cruel reason behind it. Just as he had starved out the peasant farmers, just as he had purged the Red Army and the Party itself of anyone who might be a single drop less than one hundred percent loyal to Stalin himself, the Great One had thrown whole armies and populations into the flames for reasons of his own.

Quietly, cautiously, Gagarin looked into the matter. He had to know. Know for certain. An offhand question here. A casual remark there. Never to the same person twice. Always weeks between one little probe and the next. He even secretly leafed through the daily reports of the man who had preceded him as Stalin's private secretary.

Yes, it was true. The British had warned that German troops were massing on the Soviet Union's border. Churchill himself had indeed sent a clearly worded cablegram to Stalin. Even the Americans, still neutral at that point, had warned of the impending invasion. The surprise blitzkrieg should have been no surprise at all.

The long-suppressed hatred of Stalin flamed in Gagarin's guts like a burst ulcer. With the hatred there was fear, much stronger than the hate. If he was discovered, if anyone even suspected the thoughts that were burning through his mind! Siberia, at least. Death, more likely. For Yuri too. Stalin was nothing if not thorough. Gagarin's terror made his hands shake and kept him awake at night. But if Stalin ever noticed that his private secretary was overwrought he gave no indication of it.

Gagarin also felt the pain of utter frustration, because he knew that no matter how much he hated Stalin, no matter how much he dreaded the day when Yuri would finally be old enough to go to war, there was nothing he could do. Absolutely nothing.

Until the Tehran Conference.

As the three great leaders of the anti-Nazi Allies sat in the garden of the Persian villa where they were holding their meetings, Churchill presented Stalin with the Sword of Stalingrad. Crafted by Wilkinson Steel, the Sword was a token of appreciation for the tenacious Russian defense of their nation—especially the bloody agony of the city of Stalingrad.

All the staffs of the Big Three were turned out into the garden for the ceremony. They applauded on cue as Churchill handed the heavy Sword to Stalin while Roosevelt looked on admiringly. The motion picture newsreel cameras whirred. Stalin took the Sword from its scabbard and raised it to his lips. Then he handed it to Marshal Voroshilov, Inspector General of the Red Army. Voroshilov dropped it.

A single furious glance from Stalin stopped the newsreel cameras immediately. Flustered, red-faced with embarrassment, Voroshilov picked up the Sword with trembling hands. It took him three tries to replace it in its scabbard. Finally he marched off with it, escorted by a goose-stepping honor guard. Gagarin thought the soldiers were working very hard to suppress grins at the Inspector General's mortification.

Afterward, in the privacy of his villa suite, Stalin grumbled to Gagarin, "Instead of a second front against the Nazis they give me a toy."

That evening there was a formal banquet, to which Gagarin and the others of his level were not invited. Grigori ate with the other Russian staff in the lower-floor dining room that was used for servants, then went out for a walk in the moonlit, perfumed garden.

"Comrade Gagarin," a voice whispered in the shadows.

Grigori peered into the dark shrubbery and saw the single unwinking red glow of a cigarette. A man stepped out onto the garden walk before him, gravel crunching beneath his shoes, his face masked in shadows. He was broad of shoulder, heavily built, and seemed to be wearing a soldier's tunic. More than that Grigori could not make out.

"A lovely evening, no?" said the man, in a rasping smoker's whisper. Gagarin got the impression his shadowy companion was some years older than he himself.

"Quite lovely," Grigori replied.

They strolled along the winding garden path together, smoking, speaking about the day's events.

"The Sword is a thing of beauty, is it not?"

The man had a way of turning statements into questions that unnerved Gagarin. He nodded and said nothing.

"I wish I could chop his head off with it."

Startled at the man's sudden fervor, Gagarin asked, "Whose head?"

"His. You know who."

Involuntarily, Gagarin sucked in his breath.

"I am a soldier, comrade Gagarin. Yet my family has suffered from that man's cruelty even more than your own."

"How do you know . . ." Grigori cut off his words. This man was dangerous.

"I know all about you, comrade. I have made it my business to know. And no, I am not from the secret police. They are the last people on earth I would deal with!"

Gagarin coughed on a double lungful of cigarette smoke.

Eyes watering, he said to the man; "I must get back now. Tomorrow will be a very difficult day."

"Yes. And all the other tomorrows. Until the people are rid of that murderous tyrant."

Grigori turned and started back toward the villa, but the man caught his arm and stopped him. "The Sword, comrade Gagarin. When the day comes, use the Sword."

Grigori pulled his arm free and nearly flew back to the main building. It was not until he was safely in his bed with all the lights out and the covers pulled up over his chin that he realized he had never actually seen the man's face. Nothing but the glow of his cigarette and the shadows cast by the shrubbery. He said he was a soldier.

Grigori trembled in his bed.

But once they returned to Moscow and Stalin was about to send the Sword to the War Museum, Gagarin found himself persuading his master to keep the Sword in his office. He marveled at his own audacity. Use the Sword, he said to himself, his innards quaking with fear and rage. Chop his head off with it. A small, meaningless act of defiance. Not even in his dreams did Gagarin see himself using the Sword against Stalin.

Yet he trembled. He slept poorly. He requisitioned the tape recorder to listen to his own nighttime mutterings.

That had happened sixteen months ago. He still trembled.

8

Berlin, 2 April   The long table was supported on six rough sawhorses. Three powerful lamps dangling from the bunker's concrete ceiling lit the relief model in harshly pitiless glare.

"You can see the situation quite clearly, my Führer," General Heinrici was saying. "Zhukov's First Byelorussian Army Group has established several small beachheads on the western bank of the Oder, here—" he pointed with a long stick to the tiny red flags stuck into the relief model, "—here, and here."

Hitler nodded. At his side stood Field Marshal Wilhelm Keitel, chief of staff of the *Wehrmacht,* nodding in synchrony with his Führer. Known behind his back as *lakaitel,* the lackey, Keitel's main function was to agree with Hitler under any and all circumstances. Otherwise he rarely had anything to say. His greatest recent achievement had been to sit as one of the judges of the generals who had tried to assassinate Hitler the previous July.

Across the table General Heinz Guderian scowled sourly at the relief model. The brilliant innovator who had perfected the armored blitzkrieg tactics that had crushed Poland and France, Guderian had fallen out of favor with his Führer two years earlier when he reported the truth of Germany's impending collapse on the eastern front. He had remained loyal to Hitler during the July crisis and denounced the would-be assassins, even though he had known of their plot and had not reported it. Now, with Berlin itself threatened by the advancing Russians, Guderian had been summoned back into the Führer's presence.

"Koniev's First Ukranian Army Group is about one hundred twenty kilometers to the southeast, along this front," Heinrici went on.

"And Army Group Vistula? What are your defensive dispositions?" Hitler asked, his voice low but firm.

Heinrici glanced at Keitel, who looked away. The Russians had just encircled the 20th Panzers and were in the process of shredding them into hamburger. Zhukov was consolidating his bridgeheads on the Oder's western bank and there was damned little between the Russians and Berlin.

Colonel-General Gotthard Heinrici was a practical man and a good soldier. He had bled the Russians white while retreating across the Carpathians in Silesia. But now there could be no retreat. Berlin must be defended to the last.

Turning his blunt, humorless face to his Führer, he said, "We can make them pay for every centimeter of ground they advance. But we cannot stop them. Not without massive reinforcements."

Hitler nodded and heaved a mighty sigh. "Then you shall

have them, General. Every available man. I promise this to you."

"That is very good, my Führer."

"With all respect, sir," Guderian asked from across the table, "where will these reinforcements come from? Our troops in the west are fully engaged against the British and the Americans. The same for our forces in Italy."

Hitler glared at him, then pointedly turned his back to Guderian and asked Heinrici, "What are you doing now? How long can you hold them off?"

Heinrici ran a hand across his scalp, shaved so severely that he almost looked bald. "I know Zhukov," he said, "and how he operates. He will use his superior strength in artillery to bombard our forward positions for a full day or more. Then he will launch his tanks at us in overwhelming numbers."

Hitler scowled.

"Therefore," Heinrici continued, "I will withdraw my men from the forward lines when the bombardment begins. Let Zhukov blast away at empty trenches. When the smoke clears and the tanks move in, we will reoccupy the forward positions and destroy his armor."

"Good! Excellent!" Hitler beamed and clapped his hands. "That is what we did in the trenches on the western front in the last war. Excellent!"

Heinrici felt a small glow of pleasure at having brightened his Führer's mood, even if only momentarily. Keitel smiled broadly. Guderian looked skeptical.

"Now then," said Hitler, "let me go about the work of getting you the reinforcements we need."

"My Führer," said Guderian, in a tone that could not be ignored, "it is my duty to ask the practical questions, no matter how unpleasant they may be."

Keitel began, "This is no time for such—"

"This is the *only* time we have!" Guderian shouted at the field marshal. "The Bolsheviks are attacking with two hundred divisions; more than two million men, six thousand tanks and assault guns. How can we reinforce Heinrici? Where will the troops come from? As far as I can see we have fewer than two hundred tanks available. Hardly any artillery remains. How can we reinforce Berlin with men and equipment that don't exist?"

Hitler banged his fist on the table top. "Enough! I will not listen to such defeatist talk. How dare you speak to me like that? Don't you think I am fighting for Germany? My whole life has been one long struggle for Germany! I am working night and day like a slave to save this city, to save this nation from the Bolsheviks and all you can do is raise objections. I know there are difficulties. Of course there are difficulties. You always concentrate on the problems—all of you." His eyes swept the room.

"I alone must bear all these burdens! You are no help to me. None of you understand the total situation in the way that I do."

Hitler tottered along the side of the table, one hand on its edge to keep him steady. "For more than twelve years now I have led the German people to greatness and every step of the way you generals opposed me. Don't deny it! I know it's true. When I gave the command to send our troops into the Rhineland in Nineteen Thirty-five you generals opposed me. You were frightened to march into Austria, you were crapping in your pants over the Sudetenland. But I persevered. I won! I created a greater Germany, greater than your wildest dreams. I alone!"

Keitel murmured, "Of course you did, my Führer."

"And now, now when there are difficulties, now when the whole world has turned against us, you offer me no help at all. I must plan the defense of Berlin. I must bring together the forces for the counterattack against the Bolsheviks. I alone! And what do you do? You complain and whine and wheedle. All of you!"

"My Führer," Guderian said softly, "this is not Nineteen Thirty-five. Germany is surrounded by enemies. Enemy troops are marching across German soil."

"Don't you think I know that?" Hitler roared. "I know it better than any of you. But look—look at the map! *We* hold much more of Germany than they do! I can show you, I can prove it with a ruler and compass! The amount of German territory they hold is tiny compared to the amount we still have! Tiny!"

Still on the other side of the table, Guderian asked, "But what does that matter if—"

"Traitors!" Hitler screamed. "I am surrounded by traitors and defeatists!" Pointing a wavering finger toward Guderian, "You saw the films of the July conspirators, their executions. You watched them wriggling like fish on the ends of the piano wire while their pants fell down and they crapped their guts out. It could happen to you! It could happen to any one of you! I will not have defeatists around me! I will be merciless with the traitors in my midst!"

Suddenly he stopped, panting for breath. Keitel eyed Guderian uneasily. Hitler turned away from the relief model and headed for the steel door. Keitel clicked his heels and gave the Nazi stiff-arm salute to his Führer's retreating back. Guderian stood absolutely still, his face dead white.

Once the steel door clanged shut Heinrici turned back to the model and shook his head wearily. Reinforcements? From where? Guderian was entirely right. The Führer was living in a dream world if he thought he could find enough troops to stop this avalanche of Russians.

"You should not have upset the Führer," Keitel hissed at

Guderian. "When he becomes angry like that, anything could happen."

Guderian made a bitter smile. "What's the matter, Willy? Are you afraid to die? We are all dead men already. Don't you understand that?"

9

London, 3 April   Harold Adrian Russell Philby was born in India in 1912. His father, St. John (Jack) Philby, was an arrogant dynamic man who spent a lifetime in the far reaches of the British Empire doing everything he could to confound his fellow Establishment Englishmen. It was Jack Philby who convinced King ibn-Saud to sell his oil leases not to the English, but to the upstart American oil men.

For reasons that his son never fathomed, St. John Philby detested the Establishment in London. He loathed the clubs and cliques to which he had been born. He spent his life in the heat and passion of the Middle and Far East. He nicknamed his son Kim, after the boy in Kipling's novel who was born of English parents but lived as an Indian lad.

Kipling's fictitious Kim spied for the British in India against the tsarist Russians. Kim Philby, however, lived in

London and spied for the communist Russians against the British Empire.

He was very successful at his spying, so much so that, by 1945, he was highly placed in the Establishment's own Secret Intelligence Service. He did not regard his activities for the Russians as spying, exactly. He had learned at his father's knee that men such as Churchill were snobs and racists who regarded themselves as better than other men. He had been taught at Cambridge, during his university days, that the great experiment in communism being tried in Soviet Russia was mankind's only hope for a better, more decent world.

In his deepest soul, Kim Philby was certain that Britain—the ruling Establishment class, that is—was basically fascist. The war against Hitler was not a battle of ideology but of naked power. The Establishment would not tolerate any nation acquiring enough power on the Continent to challenge the British lion. The Establishment went to war against Hitler just as they had gone to war against Napoleon: to preserve their own privileges and superiority.

Now Kim Philby sat in his office at SIS headquarters in London and pondered the two reports resting on his desk. He was a boyishly handsome man of thirty-three, with thick dark hair and a trim athletic figure. He drank a bit more than he should, and he knew it, but the alcohol and his sedentary lifestyle had not yet begun to bulge his waist. His eyes were calm and gray, the gift of his placid mother. They did not flash and simmer as his father's did; Kim kept his passions well hidden, under painstaking control. He never raised his voice. To the men around him he was a good, reliable, quiet worker. His superiors were very pleased that Kim fit in so much better than his wild-eyed, bombastic father.

The two reports on his desk were very different. One was neatly typed on official stationery with a proper security classification stamped in red at its top and bottom. The other was scrawled on a torn piece of notebook paper that Kim had picked up at a secret rendezvous in the pub down the street from SIS headquarters.

The scrawled note was difficult to decipher, but apparently one of the Soviet agents among the scientific chaps had come across something curious. He was asking for a face-to-face meeting to pass on his information. Too intricate to put into a short note.

Philby took the torn tablet page in his hand, balled it up, and tossed it into his wastebasket. Face-to-face meetings were dangerous. He had never met this agent. It was foolish to let someone see your face, especially when that someone might be working for MI5, the counter-intelligence department.

The official memorandum bothered him even more. Apparently the Yanks had made contact with Goering's people and a visit was on between the American OSS and the Reichsmarschall himself. The Foreign Office had been informed but not asked to participate.

Bloody Yanks think they can pull off a coup by themselves, Philby thought. But he knew the true significance of this message was deeper than American arrogance. Goering himself is ready to make overtures of surrender—to the Americans. Philby knew that such a surrender would automatically include the British, but not the Russians. No, the Germans are trying to work out a deal with us so they can shift all their forces against the Red Army. If I know Fat Hermann, he'll try to convince the Yanks that we should go to war against Soviet Russia.

That was important. Vitally important. Philby picked up

his telephone and called his favorite restaurant to make a dinner reservation. There he would send this crucial information on its way to Moscow. The Kremlin has got to know, he told himself. It would be just like Winnie to let the Nazis bleed the Russian armies white and then attack the Soviet Union at the first opportunity.

He still had the rest of the afternoon ahead of him, and that puzzling request for a meeting from the scientist fellow. Philby got up from his desk and went to the outer office, where he told his secretary that he would be away for an hour or two. Then he strolled down the corridor to the offices of MI5, where he asked for permission to browse through their files on an Irish agent named Finnigan. Everyone in the offices knew Philby; he was well liked and fully trusted.

Once back in the files room, Philby searched for an hour for any mention of Klaus Fuchs. There was none. Kim smiled to himself. No one knew about Fuchs. He moved to the agency's personnel files. There was nothing on Fuchs there, either. Philby's smile widened. Fuchs was not on the agency's payroll. It was safe to meet with him.

At four in the afternoon, while the rest of the office was taking tea, Kim Philby went down the street to the Crown and Shield and sat in the last booth in the back room. A slight man with a high forehead, dressed in a rather shabby suit, hesitantly approached the booth, squinting through thick rimless glasses.

"This is my favorite spot," he said, in a Middle European accent.

"There's no reason why we can't share, like good comrades," said Philby.

The password given and correctly countered, Klaus Fuchs slid into the booth. In fifteen minutes of swift whispering he revealed to Philby that a small amount of deadly plutonium had been brought to England shortly before the Tehran Conference.

"I understand," Philby said at last. "The question is: why did they do it? What was the plutonium used for?"

"Not for scientific research," Fuchs said. "That much I am certain of."

"Then what?"

"Plutonium is very dangerous. It can kill a man from its radiation after only a brief exposure."

"But your contact carried it across the Atlantic with no ill effects, you say."

"It was encased in lead. He was protected."

Philby shook his head. "I'm afraid this makes very little sense to me."

Fuchs seemed almost pathetically intense. "Don't you see? The plutonium could make a perfect assassination weapon! Silent, invisible: only a speck of it can release enough radiation to kill a man within a matter of a few days."

Oh Lord, thought Philby. Another of Winston's mad schemes to do away with Hitler. That Professor Lindemann of his.

"I see," he said to Fuchs. "Thank you for taking the risk of reporting this to me."

Fuchs wanted more, but Philby would say nothing else, certainly nothing to indicate that he would send this information on to Moscow. It's enough to meet with the man in a public place; it's quite another thing to admit in so many words that one is working for Moscow.

That evening, at his favorite restaurant, Philby passed on the vital news that the Americans were discussing a separate peace with Goering. He added, almost as an afterthought, Fuchs' story about plutonium as a possible assassination weapon.

The waiter who took his report passed it to the Soviet embassy that very evening. Before midnight the information was sent to Moscow in a coded radio message. British code-breakers had cracked the Soviet diplomatic code, of course, and the message was routinely sent the following morning to SIS headquarters, where it was just as routinely placed on the desk of Harold Adrian Russell Philby.

10

Moscow, 4 April Gagarin received his instructions in his own apartment. It terrified him.

He rarely received mail; only an occasional card or short letter from Yuri, from his school on the other side of the Ural Mountains. But when he climbed the stairs to his apartment and unlocked the door, he found an oblong white envelope on the floor waiting for him.

No return address on the envelope. An odd way to deliver a letter, slipping it under the door. Could it be from one of his neighbors in the building? They were all government employees, as he was. The envelope looked official, crisp, white, good quality paper. But no return address. Not even any postage on it. It had not gone through the post office; it had been delivered by hand.

Whose hand? Grigori's insides began to twitch as he sat himself down in his only easy chair and contemplated the letter that he had placed carefully on the end table beside him.

It was very late. Stalin had kept going with Zhukov and Koniev well past midnight, the two field marshals presenting their plans for the capture of Berlin. After hours of maps and lists and discussion that sometimes rose to the pitch of heated argument, Stalin had dismissed them both without making a decision.

Grigori felt drained, exhausted, so tired that he knew he would not be able to sleep. And there was this strange letter. Delivered by an invisible hand.

He smoked a cigarette, sitting tiredly in the beat-up old upholstered chair, trying to relax enough to feel sleepy. Dawn would be breaking soon and Stalin would expect him back in the office to start the new day within a few hours. Get some sleep, Grigori told himself. Go to bed and try to sleep.

But his hands reached out to the letter. His fingers were trembling as he tore the envelope apart and pulled out the single sheet of paper inside.

It was a letter from some woman he had never heard of, Valentina Markova. She addressed Grigori as if they were old friends. Grigori's hands shook as he realized that someone, *someone* had gone to a good deal of trouble to invent this woman and this relationship. Why? What did they want? Who was deviling him so?

With an effort of will he forced his hands to remain steady enough so he could read the letter clearly. He read it twice. Three times. It made no sense.

Markova, whoever she was (if she even existed), was telling him about a toy that she had bought for her son. A toy sword. Nonsense! snorted Grigori. Where would anyone find a toy sword these days? There was no metal for toys of any kind, not even wood; everything went to the war effort. But the letter blithely described this toy sword with a secret compartment in its hilt.

"If you take the magic jewel out of the secret compartment and hide it someplace such as a desk drawer," the letter said, "it will make your most secret dream come true. It will grant you your heart's most impossible desire. Truly it will. If you use the sword as described."

Grigori had no idea how long he sat there staring at the letter. It was written in a woman's graceful flowing hand. It was a death warrant.

At last he realized that sunlight was brightening the sky outside his one window. He lit another cigarette, got up from his chair and went into the kitchen, the letter clutched tightly in his fist. Standing at the sink, he burned the letter and its envelope, then washed their ashes down the drain.

He no longer trembled. His innards were calm. He felt almost as if he were frozen into a block of ice. Yet he moved. He undressed, splashed water on his face, shaved, combed his hair, dressed in a clean shirt and his second suit. *A death warrant*, he knew. *For both of us.*

As he walked through the cold early morning toward Red Square, the streets empty except for the old women sweeping with their straw brooms, his breath steaming in the crisp April air, Grigori heard the mysterious man at Tehran telling him to use the Sword when the time came. And the drunken Englishman from years earlier with his story about the warnings that Stalin ignored. In his mind's eye he saw once again Churchill handing Stalin the Sword of Stalingrad.

Treacherous murdering Englishman. Smiling as he handed over the weapon of assassination. They want me to be a traitor. They want me to be the hand that strikes.

The wall of the Kremlin loomed above him as he walked

past Lenin's Tomb. The ornate spires of St. Basil's Cathedral rose into the milky morning sky, glinting in the newly risen sun. As he did every morning, Grigori presented his identification card at the heavily guarded gate.

"A bit early, even for you, Comrade Gagarin," said the soldier who inspected his credentials.

Grigori had no idea that he had ever seen this man before. The guards had all been faceless soldiers to him.

How many have gone from this guard post into the front lines? he asked himself as he walked toward the Presidium building. How many faceless sons of Russia have been thrown into the meatgrinder?

It all came back to him as he entered the office complex and started up the dark wooden stairs. The starvings and deportations before the war; his own parents, half his village dead of hunger while the soldiers carried the harvest to Moscow. The blunders when the Nazis first invaded, whole armies surrounded and butchered because Stalin would not let them retreat to safer positions.

And Yuri. It all came down to Yuri. The only kin I have left in this world. Gagarin knew what Stalin was planning. He had already swallowed Poland. The plans in his desk would make him master of Eastern Europe up to the Elbe River. Then would come the move westward, to take the rest of Germany from the British and Americans, to sweep to the Channel and make all Europe a Soviet colony. Not for the betterment of the people. Not for the triumph of communism over the hated capitalists. Not even for the glory of Mother Russia.

For Stalin. For his personal power. He would sacrifice anyone, kill millions, torture hundreds of millions, to satisfy his own insane greed for power.

He will drag Yuri into his wars. Yuri will become a flier and be killed for the gratification of Stalin's lust.

Grigori saw that future as clearly as he saw the details of Stalin's office: the desk with its hidden dais, the sawed-off chairs in front of it. And the Sword of Stalingrad hanging on the wall behind it.

He knew that once he reached for the Sword, once he stepped behind the Great One's desk, his course was marked for death. He found himself standing beside the desk, knowing that at any moment Stalin might open the door and enter the office. He took a deep breath. He no longer trembled. He had made his decision.

Swiftly he moved behind the desk and took the Sword from the wall. It was heavy in his hands. No surprise that Voroshilov had dropped it. Grigori wondered how warriors of old could wield such weapons without wearying their arms within minutes.

Laying the Sword on Stalin's clear desktop, Grigori tried to unscrew the pommel. It did not open easily; he had to apply all the strength he could muster. His sweating hands kept slipping on the smooth rock crystal of the pommel. He pulled out his handkerchief and wrapped it around the crystal, which was etched with a gold Rose of England.

Finally it gave slightly, then turned in his hand. He unscrewed it and removed the pommel. The hilt seemed solid inside, until he lifted the Sword almost straight up in the air. Then a small oblong cylinder slid out and thumped on the desktop hard enough to make Grigori jump. He glanced at both doors to the office, the Sword clutched in his two hands, its blade resting on his shoulder. Nothing. No one had heard. The cylinder sat on the desktop, dark and small and heavy-looking. There was a dent in the wood where it had struck.

Feeling like a boy in a fairy tale who had just discovered the magic talisman, he put the Sword down again and unscrewed one end of the black cylinder. Inside it was a tiny wafer, almost as small as his own thumbnail.

This is the magic weapon that will slay the ogre? he asked himself. He slid the wafer out of the lead cylinder. It felt warm in his hand. Opening the top drawer of Stalin's desk, he slipped the wafer deep into its farthest reaches, under the papers that marked the course of future conquests.

His hands began to tremble again as he slid the empty lead cylinder back inside the Sword's hilt and screwed the pommel back in place. Then he lifted the Sword once more and hung it back on the wall.

It's done, he told himself as he went to his own desk and sat down. He was perspiring. Whatever that thing is, I've done what they wanted me to do. Maybe it's the voice of God telling me to smite the tyrant. He laughed to himself, bitterly. He had not thought of God or religion since his parents had died. More likely than the voice of God, he thought, he had taken his instructions from British Intelligence.

Stalin entered the office, coughing, shuffling in his bedroom slippers, and went to his desk without saying a word to Grigori. He opened the top desk drawer and began rummaging inside it. Grigori's heart stopped. What if he finds it? What if he notices the dent in the desktop? What if he was watching me?

Stalin pulled out a thick sheaf of papers. "There are a few more names I want added to this list," he said, his voice thick with phlegm this morning.

Grigori leaped up from his chair and hurried to his master's side. "Which list is that, comrade secretary?"

"The names of people to be rounded up in Hungary, once the army has cleared the Nazis out," said Stalin. "Beria thinks that we should take all the university professors who are not members of the Party. I agree."

"But that would be hundreds of men, wouldn't it, sir?"

Stalin reached for his tobacco humidor. "What difference?" he snapped, with some irritation. "If we are to set up our own regimes in these countries we can't leave intellectuals there to act as centers of opposition."

"No, I suppose not," said Grigori. He took the papers from Stalin's desk and retreated from the smell of the tobacco and the heat of the man's presence. Or was it the heat of the wafer in the desk drawer? Grigori half-thought he could see the thing through the thick wooden sides of the desk, burning away like a magic amulet of old.

11

Paris, 4 April   General Dwight David Eisenhower was angry; furious, in fact. His bald frog's face was splotched with red, he huffed and snorted and grumbled as he stood at the hotel window, looking out at the Tuileries gardens, still green and beautifully tended even after four years of Nazi occupation.

"How could he?" Eisenhower muttered. He turned to face his closest aide and confidant, General Bedel Smith. "Beetle, how in hell could he *do* this to me?"

Smith had spent the war placating British officers angered by the upstart Yanks and American officers riled by the know-it-all Brits. But now the commander of the whole kit and kaboodle was ready to kick one of their own in the backside. Hard.

"Do you know what they call him?" Eisenhower snapped, his voice brittle, testy. "Jesus Christ Himself Lee. That's what they call him."

Smith thought that J. C. H. Lee's family name was lustrous enough to stand on its own, but he kept his thoughts to himself. As usual.

Lieutenant General John C. H. Lee was in charge of the support operations for Eisenhower's headquarters. Where Ike had planned to use Paris as an R&R center for his battle wearied troops, Lee had grandly filled every hotel in the city with his own rear-echelon officers and men. Eisenhower was blazing with fury once he found out.

"I'll kick his butt all the way back to Kansas," Ike muttered. "Every GI in Europe knows that Paris has been turned into a soft deal for headquarters types. They're writing letters back home blaming *me* for this screw-up!"

Beetle Smith knew how sensitive Ike was to criticism, especially criticism from the front-line troops that made its way back to the voters in the States. Ike always denied that he was interested in going into politics after the war, but somehow these days he seemed more concerned with those mothers and fathers and wives and sweethearts back home than with polishing off the Germans.

"Let me talk to Lee," Smith suggested, walking slowly across the luxurious sitting room toward his boss at the window. "I think we can work this out without blowing it up into a major set-to."

"He's got to go," Eisenhower said firmly, shaking his head.

"He's got a lot of connections back home, you know. Might be better if you just let me work it out. We don't need to give the newspapers something like this to chew on."

Eisenhower snorted, paced away from the window. The hotel had been used by the German generals and their staffs during the occupation. Now the victorious American generals and staffs filled it. That seemed normal enough to Smith, but Eisenhower was worried about how it would look back home. Not about Montgomery and his insistence on being the star of the show, not about Bradley's increasing difficulties keeping Patton quiet, not even about Churchill's hasty mission to Washington to try to get the Berlin decision reversed. Ike was worried about the home front.

Smith figured that his boss needed some good news, something to take his mind off frying General Lee.

"G–2 has gotten wind of something interesting," he said mildly, following Eisenhower step for step across the lavish oriental carpeting.

Eisenhower said nothing, just kept pacing.

"OSS is asking Washington for permission to meet with Goering."

"What?" Eisenhower spun around.

"Looks like Fatso might be trying to cut a deal for himself."

"Where? When? Who's going to this meeting?"

Smith shook his head. "Don't know. You know these cloak-and-dagger boys. They play everything close to the vest."

"How'd G–2 hear about it?"

"That's their *business,* Ike."

"We've got to get one of our own people in on this," Eisenhower said.

"It's a little dicey," Smith answered. "If we admit that we know about it, OSS will know we've got a pipeline into their communications."

Eisenhower locked his hands behind his back, his face in that same tight-lipped expression he had worn when he made the final decision to go on June sixth despite the marginal weather.

"Beetle, we've got to work something out here. If Goering is willing to talk to the OSS, that could mean the surrender of the entire German front. We've *got* to have a man there, someone we know and trust, someone who can assess the military aspects of this situation."

Eisenhower started pacing across the room again, but now he was rattling off names, running through a list of officers who might be able to get into this meeting with the number two man of Nazi Germany.

Bedel Smith smiled to himself. He had gotten Ike off this silly business of J. C. H. Lee. Maybe, with luck, I'll even be able to get him to rethink his decision on Berlin, Smith hoped.

London, 4 April   Winston Churchill sat up in bed, alone in the little bedroom just off the war room deep below 10 Downing Street. His afternoon nap was a ritual that seldom was interrupted. Not that he slept each afternoon. Often there was too much to do, too many decisions to make. He used the siesta as an excuse to get away from all the others, away from the telephone and the messengers and the printed sheets of yellow paper that so often bore terrible tidings.

So he sat in his silk pajamas, propped by a small mountain of pillows, the bedclothes covered with a scattering of reports. A weak whiskey and water stood on the night table beside him, and the lockbox to which only he and one other man had the key sat unopened beside him. He hated this set of rooms so deep underground. Hated the thick wooden beams that supported the ceilings, hated the artificial light, the lack of sunshine and fresh air. Yet he had run the war from these rooms and he had no intention of changing now, not when things were going so well.

He read some of the reports for a while, sipping at his whiskey, trying to ignore the small red leather lockbox. The Americans were arranging a meeting with Goering, alone, without a British representative accompanying them.

Churchill's first instinct was to reach for the telephone and call Washington, but he held himself in check. No sense adding another strain to the relationship with Franklin. Let them have this meeting by themselves. If anything comes of it, we will attend the later meetings.

He started in on the other reports, but the lockbox seemed to beckon to him, to call with the softly irresistible voice of a siren. He could not concentrate on what he was reading; his eyes constantly wandered to the lockbox. With a sigh, he reached inside his pajama shirt for the key on the chain around his neck. He opened the box and adjusted his reading glasses on his nose.

There was a single sheet of paper inside. It bore a hand-lettered message. No letterhead, no department code, nothing that could be traced to any person or branch of the government.

The order has been given.

That is all that the message said. The order has been given. There was no date on the message, either, but Churchill knew it was at least two days old. Nothing new has transpired in the past forty-eight hours. The order has been given, but has it been carried out?

Relocking the leather-covered box, Churchill thought to himself, We'll know soon enough if it's been carried out. Soon enough.

What if the entire scheme backfires? It could mean a complete rupture between us and the Russians. So be it. I will take the complete blame. It will be the end of my career, worse than the Dardanelles fiasco of the last war. I'll be known to history as a failed murderer. A blunderer.

What would Franklin say? I don't mind a split with the Russians, but would the Americans break with us? That would be catastrophic. Surely Franklin will see that we must stand against Stalin sooner or later. Franklin knows by now that his "Uncle Joe" cannot be trusted. But the rest of them—Marshall and Stimson and that little man who's Vice President now. They will be shocked. Angry. Furious at my perfidy.

Churchill thought back to the early days of the war when Britain stood alone against the Nazis and he worked night and day to get America to come in and help. Franklin understood the need, but the rest of the country was dead-set against becoming involved in what they thought of as England's war.

With a shake of his head, Churchill tried to cast his mind forward. No sense mulling over the past. What will the future be like?

Europe is shattered. Hardly a city still stands intact. The Red Army looms like a colossus over the eastern half, and if Eisenhower has his way the Soviets will control everything east of the Elbe: half of Germany, half of Austria, and all the nations of Central Europe and the Balkans. Perhaps even Greece. Vienna in their grasp. Prague. Budapest and all the other ancient capitals along the Danube. Stalin had promised to allow free elections in the nations under Soviet control but Churchill saw that the Soviet dictator had no intention of keeping his promise.

He will turn Eastern Europe into a Soviet colony, Churchill told himself. And what's to stop him from moving into *our* half of Germany? From marching into France and Italy? Both those nations have huge Communist parties that will work tirelessly for Moscow.

It will mean war. Sooner or later we shall have to draw a line and try to stop them. The British Empire no longer has the strength to do it; our fight against Hitler has bled us white. There's no one else except the Americans. The Yanks against the Russians.

Churchill shuddered at the thought. Those same Americans who wanted to stay out of "England's war" will clamor for their boys to be brought home as soon as the fighting stops. The demand to demobilize their army will be irresistible; if Franklin tries to keep his army intact the Congress will destroy him.

And while the Americans are demobilizing, Churchill thought, Stalin will be taking over Eastern Europe and preparing to move westward. Then, sooner or later, we will have to fight the Communists. We will have to go through this whole bloody business all over again, just as we did with Hitler. Only worse this time, because the Russians are so much stronger.

He must be stopped. Now, before he can consolidate his grip on his winnings. If the plan fails I will take the blame. But if it succeeds . . .

Churchill's fleshy face puckered into a frown. Who will replace Stalin? The most likely candidate is Beria, the head of their secret police. He is not well loved by the other men in the Kremlin, I'm sure. But he is closest to the seat of power. Undoubtedly there will be a power struggle among them. But the chances are that Beria will win it.

Will he be just as bad as Stalin? Probably so. But will he be as *capable* as Stalin? The others will not trust him, although they will doubtless obey him out of fear.

Beria is the number two man in Soviet Russia. He is a very good number two, by all the reports we have had of him. But how good a number one man would he make?

Churchill leaned his head back against the pillows and stared sightlessly at the heavy beams supporting the ceiling. Number two men rarely make great leaders. Goering would be nowhere as powerful or effective as Hitler is. Even Eden, good man that he is, could not possibly be as strong a Prime Minister as I. He simply hasn't the stomach for it. And Franklin's number two, that little man Truman, I should hate to see what a mess he would make if ever he became President.

Churchill reached out a hand and patted the lockbox as if it were an affectionate grandchild. Broadsword is the answer, he told himself. Whether it works or not it will get the job done. The only question is, how many of us will it take down to ignominy along with Stalin?

12

Burg Valdenstein, 6 April   Despite himself, Allen Dulles whistled aloud as the open car climbed the last section of winding road. General Wolff, sitting beside him, allowed a wintry smile to cross his face.

"It's like a castle out of a Grimm Brothers tale," Dulles said.

"Just so," said Wolff. "Burg Valdenstein is nearly a thousand years old. It has withstood many invaders over the centuries. It is the Reichsmarschall's home, since he was a little boy."

It wasn't a huge place, Dulles saw as they came nearer. But there were the stone turrets and battlements, arrow-slit windows, even a wooden bridge across an empty moat.

The two big blond types that had come with Wolff to Switzerland were up front, one of them driving the heavy Mercedes, both in their regular black SS uniforms. Wolff was still in mufti and Dulles in his usual tweed jacket and casual slacks. He clutched his snap-brim fedora with one hand to keep the wind from whisking it away; Wolff had on a tweed cap that matched his suit. It was a beautiful April morning, bright with sunshine and sweet with blooming flowers. A bit chilly in the back seat of the open Mercedes, especially when the road cut through the deep shade of the mountainside forests. But once they were in the sun again it felt fine, bracing, the kind of a day when great things can be accomplished.

They had started out from Berne as soon as Dulles had gotten the go-ahead from Washington for this meeting with Goering. Eisenhower's headquarters wanted to send one of their G–2 people, but Washington had nixed that, thank god. Bad enough to have the top OSS man in Europe waltz into Nazi Germany in the company of a clutch of SS; it would be stupid to hand them an Army G–2 man as well.

Dulles ran his tongue across the poison capsule lodged between his right molars and his cheek. Cyanide. Just in case. But Goering had a reputation for being an honorable man—for a Nazi. He had been a top fighter pilot during World War I. He had helped Jews to get out of Germany once Hitler's intentions about them became clear. Of course, the Jewish families had to leave all their possessions behind when they fled. And of course they signed over all their wealth to Hermann Goering, in thanks for being allowed to leave with their skins still in one piece.

A big open gate loomed in front of them and the car passed through the deep chilling shadow of the walled castle entrance. Then they came out into a sunny courtyard. Standing at the top of the steps of the main building stood Hermann Goering, in a powder-blue tunic heavy with medals and decorations over a pair of salmon-pink riding britches. His boots were shined to a mirror finish. His broad face was wreathed in a smile of welcome.

The car pulled up and even before it came to a full stop the SS man on the right leaped out and opened the rear door. Wolff stepped out first, then Dulles slid across the leather upholstery and climbed to his feet for the first time in nearly six hours.

To his surprise, Goering was not much taller than Dulles himself. He had expected a much bigger man. Goering was wide in the shoulders, heavy-set, although he seemed much leaner than earlier photographs had indicated. Dulles wondered to himself, If the Reichsmarschall is only this tall, then Hitler must be a real shrimp.

Although Dulles spoke passable German, Wolff introduced the two men in English. Goering took Dulles' proffered hand in both of his, tightly, like a drowning man grasping at a life preserver.

"I am delighted to meet you," Goering said in barely accented English. "I am very glad that you decided to meet with me. And even more glad that no American fighter planes were strafing the roads this morning!" He laughed heartily.

The Reichsmarschall radiated sincerity, which put Dulles on his guard even more than he would normally have been. Very tricky undercurrents here, he told himself.

Instead of plunging into the discussions that he had come for, however, Goering insisted on giving the American a tour of his castle home. He was obviously very proud of it, and he walked Dulles through every room like a real estate salesman showing a property to a prospective buyer. Dulles recognized paintings and sculptures from the cream of Europe's collections: Degas, Renoir, Cranach, Durer. He sighed to himself. I suppose if Goering hadn't stolen them the Nazis would have destroyed what they call decadent art works.

The Reichsmarschall looked healthy and fit; not slim, of

course, his build was too stocky for that. But the rumors of his being addicted to morphine seem to be exaggerated, at least, Dulles thought. Goering's voice boomed through the high-ceilinged rooms, enthusiastic, authoritative, very much in command.

Finally Goering ushered him and General Wolff into the dining hall, where the gleaming long table was set for three. Waiters in forest-green livery stood at attention along the paneled wall, beneath a row of antlered elk and deer heads.

"I had wanted Kesselring to join us," Goering said, gesturing Dulles to the chair at his right, "but it wouldn't do to have too many prominent men here at the same time." He laughed again. Too heartily, Dulles thought.

Dulles started to talk about the war, but Goering interrupted him to have the wine steward pour a straw-colored wine into their gleaming crystal glasses. Then the waiters served the fish course.

"Trout from the local streams," Goering said. "One of the many unfortunate aspects of this war is that it is very difficult to get good salmon."

"I've come here to see if we might be able to end this senseless fighting," said Dulles, determined to get to the subject.

Goering probed at his fish with a fork. "Senseless to you, perhaps," he muttered, not looking up from his plate. "We, however, are fighting for the very life of our Fatherland."

"It's hopeless, you know." Dulles had wanted his words to sound sympathetic; they came out like a threat.

"The Führer does not think so. He believes a miracle will happen."

Dulles glanced at Wolff, who was busily attending to the food in front of him. Even an SS general doesn't eat this well every day, he realized.

To Goering, he asked, "Do you believe in miracles?"

The Reichsmarschall smiled ruefully. "I used to. I had great faith in Hitler. We were comrades together. I was badly wounded in Nineteen Twenty-three, you know."

The infamous Beer Hall Putsch, Dulles thought. Too bad the police hadn't killed Hitler then and there.

"I never wanted this war." Goering leaned his massive body toward Dulles. "Ask anyone. I tried with all my might to prevent it. Ribbentrop and that gang of pissers, they brought this calamity upon us! Even after the fighting started I tried to get the English to see reason, to agree to an honorable peace."

Dulles asked mildly, "And what kind of a peace do you want to agree to now?"

Goering sat back in his chair, as if affronted by such a direct question. But abruptly his fleshy face broke into a boyish grin. "Yes, yes. You are right. The past is gone and cannot be changed. The future is the only thing we can deal with. Only the future."

Dulles took a taste of the trout. It was poached to delicate perfection.

"For us to continue to fight each other is foolish," said Goering. "No, worse. It is madness. There is no further reason for the United States and Great Britain to remain at war against Germany."

"What do you propose?"

"That we make common war on our common enemy: the barbarian hordes of Bolshevik Russia!"

"The Russians are our allies," Dulles said. "You can't expect our people to change sides."

With a ponderous shake of his head, Goering said, "You will end up fighting Stalin and his Asian hordes sooner or later. That is certain. The only question is, will you have

Germany fighting alongside you, or will you allow Germany to be totally destroyed before the Russian dogs turn on you?"

Dulles had no answer, so he said nothing. He turned his attention back to the food on his plate, using his knife and fork to keep his hands busy, a substitute for his pipe. Wolff sat silently across the table; not entirely silently, he was mopping up the last morsels of the fish course.

"At the very least," Goering said, with growing impatience, "you could disengage the American and British armies and allow us to move our troops to the eastern front. We will face the Russians alone, if we must."

Putting his fork down on the bone china dish, Dulles said, "Our policy is unconditional surrender. We can't—"

"I know your policy! It's nonsense! You can't expect the German people to surrender unconditionally. You're just forcing us to fight on, even when all hope has gone!"

"Are you willing to surrender to General Eisenhower?"

"I am willing to negotiate an end to hostilities on the western and Italian fronts. *Provided* that the German troops can keep their arms and be moved to the east to protect their homeland against the invading Russians."

"A separate peace with the United States and Great Britain," Dulles said.

"Yes."

"And France."

"And the damned French too. Yes."

"Will Hitler accept such a deal?" asked Dulles.

Goering reached into his tunic pocket and pulled out a handful of pills. He popped them into his mouth and reached for his glass of wine. Paracodeine pills, Dulles knew. He swills them by the hundred.

"The Führer's main concern is to protect the German people against the barbaric Russians," Goering said at last.

"That is why he is staying in Berlin, to personally lead the battle against the Bolsheviks."

"Does he know what you're discussing with me?"

Goering seemed to stiffen. "I believe that I can convince him to accept the terms I have just proposed."

"But he doesn't know you're meeting with me."

"Not yet." Goering scowled like a sullen little boy who had just been caught doing something naughty.

"He doesn't know anything about the deal you're proposing."

The Reichsmarschall took a deep breath, then forced a sickly smile. "My dear Mr. Dulles: I am not worried about the Führer. As I have told you, we are old comrades and I can speak to him frankly whenever I wish to. But I am taking a certain amount of risk in meeting with you. If Himmler knew of it, or even his assistant Bormann, I might be placed under house arrest before I could get to the Führer. Isn't that true, Wolff?"

The SS general nodded somberly.

"But you're the number two man in the Reich," Dulles probed.

"Legally, that is true. However, Himmler is in command of the SS, which has become an army of its own. He has power. All I have is legitimacy."

"I see," murmured Dulles. A real nest of snakes, he said to himself. But maybe we can get them fighting each other, if nothing else.

Goering waved a hand and the waiters began to remove the dishes. The door to the kitchen opened and the aroma of roast pork filled the stone-walled dining hall.

13

Wurzburg, 6 April   Less than sixty-five miles west of Burg
                    Valdenstein, Major Heinz Renquist
stood at the edge of the trees on the hilltop and peered
through his binoculars across the River Main. He could see
the dark brown humps of American tanks moving on the
other side of the river. Shermans. Poor tanks, undergunned
and lightly armored. No match for our Tigers, he knew. But
there were so many of them! The Americans were like a
tidal wave, overwhelming the army and its Panzers like the
ocean sweeping everything before it as it rushes up onto a
beach.

Two months ago Renquist and his Panzer unit had been
at the Saar, near the border with France. The Americans
had punched across the river and driven them back across
the sacred soil of the Fatherland. Two weeks ago they had
crossed the Rhine, a barrier that Renquist thought his
Panzers could hold indefinitely. But the Americans had

captured a bridge stupidly left intact and had poured across the best natural defense line in the region.

Now they were at the Main. They had taken Frankfurt and were about to assault Wurzburg. Renquist had three tanks left in running condition, no spare parts, and precious little petrol.

And an order from Berlin in his tunic pocket: *All available men and equipment will be moved under cover of darkness to Berlin.* The order was signed by the Führer himself.

Renquist put his field glasses down and rubbed his tired eyes. It had been a week since he'd had a bath; it seemed like years since he'd slept one whole night through.

All available men and equipment, he thought. I have no available men or equipment. I don't even have enough to cover the front I've been assigned. What does Berlin expect me to do, create fresh troops and tanks out of thin air? Or perhaps I should send the burned-out shells of my ruined tanks to them. You see, my Führer, this one was Max's. It was hit by rockets from an American P–47 *jabo.* And this one, sir: Karl and his entire crew were roasted alive in this one.

Renquist shook his head wearily. It's hopeless. It's all so hopeless. I have nothing to send to Berlin. I have almost nothing to put against the Americans.

"Sir!"

The major turned to see his aide, a teenaged sergeant, blond and pink-cheeked and looking frightened.

"Sir, there are *jabos* in the air. You should not stand so close to the clearing where they can see you."

Renquist turned and tousled the boy's hair. "Not to worry, sergeant. The Amis haven't taken to strafing individual men yet. They're still looking for tanks and trucks." And mules and horses, he added silently. Anything that moves and carries supplies or ammunition.

"The men are ready to move, sir. They are waiting for your orders."

Planting his fists on his hips and trying at least to look like the leader of a Panzer fighting unit, Renquist took in a deep breath of the tree-sweetened air. Soon, he knew, this forest would reek of cordite and torn bleeding flesh.

"Send a runner into the nearest town and find someone who knows where are the fords across the river. That is where the Americans will try to cross. That is where we must meet them."

The boy dashed off, leaving Renquist alone once more. He realized that he had said "meet" the Americans, not "stop" them. Three Tigers against an army. He shook his head and thought, I hope they don't destroy the brewery when they get to Wurzburg. That would be a shame.

On the western bank of the Main River, Lieutenant General George S. Patton, Jr. put down his field glasses and turned to his aide.

"Is that town over there Wurzburg?"

The aide, a newly minted captain fresh from the States, ran a finger down the map he was holding. He looked up, smiling, "Yessir. Wurzburg."

"They make good beer in Wurzburg. Used to, anyway, before the war. See that none of the men get themselves lost in there when we take the town. Put a cordon of MPs around the brewery."

"Yessir." The captain fumbled awkwardly, trying to write a note on his pad without putting down the map.

Patton stared across the river, the heavy field glasses hanging from the strap around his neck. His eyes were baggy, watery-looking. His mouth turned down at the corners. The polished steel helmet he wore had the three stars of his rank emblazoned on it, and the pair of ivory-handled pistols buckled around his hips proclaimed that this was truly Old Blood and Guts. He still wore cavalry-style jodhpurs and calf-length boots, caked with mud.

The captain stirred uneasily. "Uh, general . . . you make a mighty good target, sir, for any snipers that might be left in the area."

"Bullshit!" Patton snapped, in his high shrill voice. "If there're any snipers left in this area they're welcome to take a shot at me. How do you expect to instill confidence in your men if you don't show any confidence in them yourself?"

The captain fell silent and the general turned his attention to the river once again. It was a lovely April afternoon, a little warm, but dry and bright. He heard the roar of airplane engines and looked up to see a flight of P–47s thunder by, low enough to shakes leaves off the trees.

"Go get 'em flyboys!" Patton yelled, both fists raised high, his thin voice almost cracking. "Pound the shit out of 'em!"

Then he realized that the captain was flat on his face, map and notepad scattered to the breeze.

"For Chrissake," Patton screeched at him, "there aren't any Kraut planes left! You hear planes, they're ours! Understand? And even if they're not I don't want any officer of mine acting like a damned fool coward. Understand me?"

The captain, white-faced, clambered to his feet. "Y-Yes-sir."

Patton snorted with disdain. This fool won't last long. I'll have to put him in the line and see whether he makes a man of himself or gets himself killed.

He looked across the river again, seeing far beyond the horizon. To Berlin. There's nothing on the other side of that river that can stop me, he told himself. I can make a dash to Berlin just like I made the dash across France. If only Ike will let me. Instead of leaving it to the goddamned Russians, I can take Berlin. I can do it! I know I can. God didn't let me come this far just to leave the biggest prize of all to those godless communist sonsofbitches.

If only Ike would listen to reason.

Abruptly, he turned away and started back toward his jeep, where a driver waited together with a sergeant carrying a Thompson submachine gun. The captain scurried after the striding general.

"Get on the two-way and find out where General Bradley is. I've got to see him right away. Get a plane ready for me."

They piled into the jeep and were off in a cloud of dust.

One hundred sixty air miles to the north, Field Marshal Sir Bernard Law Montgomery stood on the western bank of the river Weser and peered through his field glasses at the city on the other side.

"That's Hamelin town?" he asked.

Major General Francis de Guigand replied with a smile, "Yes, it is. The Pied Piper has fled, though, and the rats still infest the the city. Rather large rats, with swastikas on their armbands, you know."

Montgomery was a little bantam cock of a man, perky, with sparkling bright eyes and a tan beret perched jauntily on his head. He wore a turtleneck sweater with no indication of his rank visible. None was needed. Everyone in the world recognized Monty on sight; he was more famous than most cinema stars. De Guigand, his chief of staff since Montgomery had taken command of the Eighth Army at El Alamein, had seen Monty rise to the position of chief of all Allied ground forces in the European Theater of Operations. But it was a virtually meaningless title rather than an actual position of power. Eisenhower and the Yanks were running the show and they knew it. This rankled Monty more each day.

"Be a shame to flatten the town," Monty said.

"Rather."

"Still, it can't be helped. If Jerry is holed up in there, we'll have to pry him out."

"Artillery?"

"By all means. A good pounding. The tanks can cross upriver and take what's left from the rear."

"Right."

Clasping his hands behind his back, Monty turned away from Hamelin town and began walking slowly back to his staff car.

"Do you realize how close we are to Berlin?"

"Less than two hundred miles, I should say," de Guigand replied.

"Yes, quite right. I could cover that distance in a week, you know. Ten days, at most."

De Guigand hesitated. As an Englishman he wanted to have Britain gain this ultimate triumph. Britain had been at war for more than five years now. At one time Britain stood totally alone against Hitler, had borne the brunt of the Nazi fury and survived it. Now victory was so close he could taste it, and Eisenhower had decreed that it would be the Russians who would be allowed to take Berlin.

"A bold, full-blooded thrust," Montgomery said, shaking a clenched fist in the air. "We could do it, man! I could do it!"

"If Ike let you," said de Guigand.

"Eisenhower," Montgomery said with disgust. "He's no general. Not a fighting general. Never was and never will be. A bloody politician, that's all he is."

De Guigand said nothing.

"I can take Berlin. Winston knows I could."

"It's the logistics, Monty. You know that. Ike would have to bring his own Americans to a halt and give you every bit of petrol and ammo he has. He won't stop Bradley's forces. He can't, actually, not without having Washington come down on him like a ton of bricks."

"But Berlin, for god's sake!"

"It's going to the Russians, Monty. Put it out of your mind."

"Never! I haven't come all the way from El Alamein to have the history books say I failed to reach Berlin."

De Guigand sighed inwardly. You know the bloody war's over when generals begin to worry about how they will appear in the history books. But then, he thought, Monty was worrying about the history books at El Alamein, and even before.

14

St. Affrique, 11 April   "Y'know," said Private Loller, "there must be a special three-star general back in the Pentagon that picks out the worst places on Earth to put army bases."

Sergeant Nick Hollis looked up from the boots he was polishing. "What's the matter, Loller? Don't you like it here?"

From across the tent, Kaplan sing-songed, "Oh, I love it here. I love the army. I never had it so good."

Loller lay back on his bunk, a soft-faced youngster with the hard cynical eyes of a combat veteran, and laced his fingers together behind his head, looking up at the dull khaki fabric of the tent billowing slightly in the breeze.

"Yeah, I can just see that lard-assed general back there in Washington: 'Where can I find a place in all of France that's infested with flies, covered with dust, is hot by day and cold at night, and as far as possible from Paris? *That's* where I'll put the Hundred and First!' "

"You couldn't get into Paris anyway," said Sanderson, stretched on the bunk next to Loller's. "The fuckin' officers have it all sewed up for themselves. Rear echelon types. No fighting units allowed in, they might mess up the Mona Lisa or something."

Jarvick, as usual, had his nose buried in the latest issue of *Stars and Stripes* that he could find. But he put the paper down and said, "The hell with Paris. I'd like to get to Arles, where Van Gogh painted. It's not all that far from here."

"Van who?"

"Van Gogh. Vincent Van Gogh."

"Who's he?"

"An artist. A painter."

"What'd he paint? Houses or outhouses?"

Jarvick gave them all a sour look and went back to his newspaper.

"Drop your socks and grab your cocks!" a voice bellowed from just outside the tent flap.

"Holy cow!"

"Kinder!"

A sawed-off, thickset man with a homely face ducked into the tent. A huge bulge distended his jaw and he was grinning from ear to ear.

"Kinder!" They all bunched around him, pounding him on the back, pumping his hand.

"You're back!"

"How're the feet?"

"I thought they'd send you back to the States."

Staff Sergeant Alven Kinder looked around for a place to spit, stuck his head out the tent flap momentarily, then rejoined his platoon mates.

"They saved all my toes, so they didn't have to send me

home," he said. "McAuliffe himself pinned a bronze star on me and sent me back to take care of you poor slobs."

"You can have 'em," Hollis said with real fervor. He had been acting squad leader since Kinder had been sent to hospital with badly frostbitten feet after Bastogne.

Hollis felt an almost overwhelming wave of gratitude that Kinder had returned to take the responsibility off his hands. He noticed Jarvick watching him, his face serious, somber. Hollis grinned at him. So I'm a grasshopper, he said to himself. I like being a grasshopper.

Sergeant Kinder took one of the empty bunks. Four months after the Bulge, half the bunks were still unoccupied. The 101st Airborne had held Bastogne even though totally surrounded. When the Germans demanded surrender, General McAuliffe replied with a single word: "Nuts." Since the end of the battle, the division had been quartered in rest-and-recuperation camps far from the fighting.

"So what's going on outside?" Jarvick asked. "We've been stuck here and they don't tell us anything."

Kinder shook his head, still lopsided from his plug of tobacco. "Well, you're all getting medals, for one thing . . ."

"Goodie," said Kaplan, acidly. "Then we'll all be official heroes."

"We got the unit citation last month," Hollis said.

"Yeah, but these'll be individual decorations," Kinder said. "Bronze stars, purple hearts. I hear there's even a couple of silver stars coming up. There's talk of Eisenhower himself coming down here to hand them out."

"I don't like it," Hollis grumbled. "Why don't they send us home and decorate us there?"

Kinder's grin faded. "There's a whole truck convoy of replacements comin' in."

"Oh-oh."

"They're gonna bring the division back up to full strength."

"Christ, haven't we done enough fighting?" Loller snapped. "What the hell do they want from us?"

"Hey, you dogfaces are famous, what more do you want?" Kaplan wisecracked.

"I want to go home!"

"Amen, brother."

Kinder shook his head like a disappointed schoolteacher whose students had failed his test. "You know what they say: the shortest road back to the States—"

"Is through Berlin," they all chorused back at him. To a man, they razzed their returned staff sergeant with the fervor that only combat veterans can muster.

15

Moscow, 11 April   A week had gone by since Gagarin had
                   placed the mysterious wafer from the
Sword into Stalin's desk drawer. A horrible, terrifying
week.

The Great One was dying. That seemed painfully clear.
He had lost so much weight so suddenly that his marshal's
tunics hung on him like bags on a scarecrow. His iron-gray
hair was falling out in patches; even his mustache seemed
frayed and ragged. He shambled when he walked, he
seemed exhausted, utterly weary. His mind wandered. He
muttered confusedly, often in his native Georgian tongue.

Whatever the source of the wafer's magic, its power had
caught Gagarin, too. He ached in every joint of his body.
His gums bled and his teeth felt loose. His hands were
blistered as though they had been burned. He dared not go
to a doctor; he bought salve and did the best he could for

himself. He too had lost weight, but not as much as his older master.

We are both dying, Gagarin told himself. It is just as well. I am killing him, and the act of it is killing me.

Stalin had still not decided whether Zhukov or Koniev would lead the assault on Berlin. For the past week the armies in the field had stopped their headlong advances. As Zhukov had wished, they were being resupplied, the weary men given a brief respite before the final battle for the Nazi capital.

No one dared to comment on the sudden deterioration of the Man of Steel. But one week to the day after Grigori had placed the wafer in Stalin's desk, he received a memorandum from Beria, asking that the subject of "cooperative leadership arrangements for the post-war period" be placed on the agenda for the meeting of the Council of Ministers scheduled for the next morning.

When Gagarin showed the memo to Stalin, the Great One merely nodded and grunted. Then he added, "The meeting will take place in my conference room, here. Not in the ministers' chamber. And only the inner cabinet, not the entire crowd of them."

"Yes, sir," said Gagarin. He knew how tired and aching Stalin felt. He felt it himself.

The inner cabinet consisted of four men: Beria, Georgi Malenkov, Viachislav Molotov, and Nikita Khrushchev. Plus Stalin, of course, who sat at the head of the table in the small, stuffy conference room.

Gagarin sat at his usual tiny desk in the corner, taking the minutes of the meeting. It hurt his blistered hand to grip the pencil. They droned through problems of steel production, grain planting schedules for the collective farms, intelligence reports on Japanese activities in Manchuria.

A ghost of a smile crossed Stalin's pockmarked face. "I

want those factories in Manchuria," he muttered. "Once we enter the war against Japan, those factories are to be dismantled and carted back inside the Soviet Union."

Khrushchev scribbled a note on the yellow pad in front of him.

They asked about the progress of the war. Stalin assured them all was well. Berlin was within reach. "Zhukov and Koniev are both dying to be the first into Hitler's capital." He started to laugh, but it ended as a hacking cough. The Man of Steel pulled out a handkerchief and brought it to his lips as he tried to control the coughing fit. The handkerchief came away bloody.

"You need a doctor, comrade secretary," said Beria, in his soft near-whisper.

"No. I will be all right."

"But . . ."

"No doctor," Stalin said, a hint of the old iron in his rasping voice. "Continue with the meeting."

For a long moment there was utter silence. Grigori could hear Stalin's labored breathing in the stillness of the room.

Then Beria, with a glance at the others around the table, said, "We should discuss leadership arrangements for the post-war period."

Stalin leaned back in his chair and reached for the pipe that had rested unlit in the massive steel ashtray on the table before him.

"What do you have in mind?" he asked.

Beria gave an uneasy smile and said, "I believe Comrade Khrushchev has been working on this matter."

Was Beria in on the English scheme? The sudden thought startled Gagarin. Was he working with the British, or allowing the British to proceed with their assassination plot, in the expectation of assuming power himself? Or was it Khrushchev, or one of the others? This plot with the Sword could not possibly have gotten so far if someone high in power were not a part of it. Grigori was instantly convinced of that. What if all of them were in on it, all of them working to murder the Great One, using poor Grigori as their cat's paw just as the British were doing? His head swam with the thought of it; he felt giddy, knowing that whatever happened, he would not outlive his dying master.

Nikita Khrushchev cleared his throat before speaking. It was his habit. Always that dreadful animal gargling noise before the words came out. He was totally bald and unhandsome. His ears stuck out, his smile showed gaps between his teeth. His eyes were tiny and almost hidden in folds of flesh. The suit he wore was baggy, rumpled, undecorated except for a single Hero of the Soviet Union medal he wore on his lapel. He had served as a political commissar with the army and seen the crushing early defeats that had been inflicted by the Nazis turned slowly, agonizingly into blood-soaked victories. Of all the men at the conference table, he had seen the most action in the field. He was closest to the commanders of the Red Army.

He cleared his throat again, like a peasant nervously appearing before a magistrate, then began:

"Comrade Secretary, once the war is ended in glorious victory—thanks to your brilliant and tireless leadership—there will be enormous tasks facing us. We will have to rebuild the areas devastated by the invaders. We will have to move our economy from a wartime basis to a peacetime one, and begin to give our people some of the fruits of the victory they have sacrificed so much to attain. We will have to demobilize our vast armies and bring the men into the peacetime economic structure—"

"No," said Stalin.

Khrushchev fell as silent as if a bullet had pierced his brain.

"The army will not be demobilized. We must be prepared to defend Eastern Europe against the capitalists. And Manchuria. Iran too, perhaps."

"But surely some demobilization will take place," Khrushchev said. "Workers will be needed to rebuild and to move the economy from war production to civilian goods."

Stalin shook his head. Gagarin saw that his face was shining with perspiration.

Malenkov, fat and soft-looking, said, "Of course, we could import labor from Poland and Romania and the rest. We also have millions of German prisoners."

"The point is," Khrushchev went on, impatiently, "that no one expects you to bear all these burdens almost single-handed, Comrade Stalin, as you have borne the burdens of the war. Once victory has been achieved, it will be a time for you to rest, comrade, to enjoy the glory and the love of your adoring people, to put down some of the burdens that . . . you . . ."

Khrushchev's voice faded and died away. Stalin was glowering at him: pale, terribly weak, sweating with pain, yet the Man of Steel silenced Khrushchev with nothing more than a glaring look.

"So you want to take over my duties, do you?" Stalin's voice was low, murderous.

"No!" Khrushchev squeaked. "That's not what I meant at all. That is—"

"And the rest of you? Do you all agree that I should be put out to retirement, like a spavined horse or an aged bull?"

No one dared to say a word.

Without bothering to turn to look at Gagarin, Stalin asked, "Who placed this subject on the agenda?"

Grigori, seated in his corner behind the Great One, stared

at Beria. Behind his pince-nez the MGB chief's eyes were wide with fright.

"Well?" Stalin roared, with something like his old fury.

"It was Comrade Beria, sir," Grigori answered in a child's guilty whisper.

Stalin gave Beria a look of contempt. "You too, Lavrentii Pavlovich? You also want me to step down?"

"No, of course not," Beria replied smoothly. "Comrade Khrushchev misunderstood the matter entirely. I would never even consider your retirement, Comrade Secretary. The people wouldn't hear of it. You are their father! Their leader! They would be lost without you."

Trembling, Stalin pushed himself to his feet. He leaned both fists on the table top and stared angrily at Khrushchev.

"You believe that the army gives you power, Nikita, don't you? Well, let me tell you something about power."

He stopped, took a deep breath. Khrushchev had pulled his head down between his shoulders, as if expecting a beating. Dour-faced Molotov, who had been curiously silent through the whole meeting, actually slid his chair slightly away from Khrushchev's.

Stalin raised one fist in the air, opened his mouth to speak. But no words came out. He waved his fist for a moment, then clutched at his chest and collapsed on the table top, his head making a crunching sound when it hit the gleaming mahogany. Before any of the men could react, Stalin's body slid to the floor with a soft thump.

Beria was the first to move. He knelt by the fallen man and took one wrist in his hand, feeling for a pulse.

"Is he dead?" Molotov asked in a whisper.

Beria shook his head. "Not yet. Gagarin! Call the doctors. Quickly."

Grigori picked up the phone and dialed the medical office. "The General Secretary has collapsed!" he shouted, surprised at the strength of his own voice. "Send his doctors immediately to the conference room!"

Khrushchev had come around the table. He bent over the prostrate form of Stalin. "He looks in a bad way."

"Yes," said Beria.

"Perhaps the doctors can save him," Molotov said.

"I doubt it," Beria replied. Gagarin realized that although Khrushchev had strong ties with the Red Army, the Kremlin medical unit reported to Lavrentii Beria.

No one in the Kremlin slept that night. The rest of Moscow knew nothing of Stalin's collapse. The army commanders, the soldiers in the field, the rest of the world were not told. There were rumors, of course. But in the wartime capital, blacked out on the information front almost as totally as the streets were blacked out against enemy bombers each night, rumors could move only slowly. Even the rumor of Stalin's death.

At two in the morning Beria called a meeting of the full Council in the big ministers' meeting chamber. Weak, shaking inside, racked with pain, Grigori Gagarin took his customary place at the long side table among the other sleepy-eyed and grumbling secretaries who each took down the minutes for their various ministers.

The meeting was very brief. Beria took the chair at the head of the polished conference table and announced that Josef Stalin had died of a stroke. Shocked silence, absolute and complete. It seemed to stretch for hours. Beria finally resumed speaking, assuring the ministers that the Party and the government would go on without the Great One. If there was any suspicion of foul play, none was mentioned. The government would be run by a committee of four: Beria, Molotov, Khrushchev and Malenkov. Each of the ministers expressed shock, grief, unending sorrow. Each went home, so Gagarin thought, wrapped in a whirlpool of fear and uncertainty—yet he thought he sensed relief, also, that the tyrant was dead.

More likely it was his own feelings that he was projecting onto the others.

If Beria or the others suspected anything, they gave no hint of it. Grigori felt no triumph in his success, no sense of exhilaration. Perhaps I've saved Yuri, he thought. That was the best he could hope for. He knew he was dying, too. He felt sick at heart, unclean, as if something was eating his body and soul from within. He knew he had been used as a weapon against the leader of his country, but used by whom? The English, or Beria, or one of the others? More likely all of them, acting together. What did it matter? He had just murdered a man; a monstrous man, perhaps, but a human being nonetheless. Now it was time to finish the job.

He went back to Stalin's office after the Council of Ministers meeting. Two of Beria's uniformed guards were at the door, but they let Gagarin through after he showed his identification and explained that he had to sort out the Great One's papers.

He dared not lock the door for fear that the click of the bolt would alert the guards and make them suspicious. But once the door was shut behind him Grigori went straight to the desk. Wrapping his blistered hand in his handkerchief, he removed the heavy dark wafer from the drawer and replaced it in the cylindrical lead container inside the Sword's hilt. The wafer seemed hot to the touch, almost glowing, even through the handkerchief. As he hung the Sword back on the wall he thought, That's the most I can do to protect you, Yuri. Unless they take the Sword apart and examine it, they will never know what I did. Even after

I'm dead, they'll have no reason to arrest you. My final act, little brother. May you live long and in peace, Yuri.

Then Grigori Gagarin left Stalin's office for the final time. Bundled in his fur-lined coat against the night cold, he left the Kremlin through the gate he always used and headed home toward his apartment block.

Tanks were rumbling through the streets. Taking up positions on Red Square, Grigori thought. But no. As he walked out onto the square he saw that they were clanking past Lenin's Tomb and heading off into the district where the ministers' apartment buildings stood. For protection? Why would the ministers need the Army's protection? Grigori felt a shudder of confusion wash through his pain-racked body.

A few flakes of snow were sifting down through the pools of light from the street lamps. There was virtually no wind. Dawn would be breaking in another hour. Grigori walked out onto the Moskvoretskii Bridge and stared down at the dark swirling ice-cold water. For long minutes he stood there gazing into the empty darkness, his body racked with pain, his soul in even worse torment. But then he thought of Yuri again and knew there was one final act he had to accomplish.

16

Berlin, 13 April   Josef Goebbels rushed so fast through the dank concrete corridors that he almost tripped himself on his club foot. He was a little man, gauntly thin, cheekbones protruding, eyes gleaming as though fevered. As Minister of Information for the Third Reich, he had not been able to bring good news to his Führer for many, many months.

Today was very different.

Hitler was in his situation room, as usual, sitting on a high stool bending over the relief map of the city. General Heinrici was with him and a few of Himmler's SS dolts. Eva Braun had apparently just stepped into the room from the door that led to the Führer's private quarters. She was an odd one, Goebbels thought: not bright at all, yet she seemed to have some sixth sense about her. She always managed to be present when there was momentous news.

"My Führer!" Goebbels fairly shouted as he hurried toward the map table.

Hitler turned, his face as gray as the uniform he wore, his eyes bleary.

"My Führer, Stalin is dead! The monster has died! Rejoice!"

"Stalin, you say?"

"Yes! Yes!" Goebbels was almost prancing with joy. "The Bolshevik devil is roasting in hell."

Hitler climbed down stiffly from his stool. He seemed more shaken by the news than elated. "Stalin. Dead."

"Yes, my Führer," said Goebbels. "The Russians have not released the news to their own people yet, but our agents have gotten the word to us and the Swedish embassy has confirmed it. He died last night, of a stroke."

"Strange," mused Hitler, stepping toward Goebbels almost as if sleepwalking. "Of the three of them, I would have thought Roosevelt would be the first to die. Cripples don't live as long as healthy men."

General Heinrici had come around the map table, his hard-bitten features looking wary, distrustful. "Is this report reliable?" he asked.

"Completely," said Goebbels. "The man is dead. I would think that there will be considerable confusion in the Russian ranks, at least for the next few days, perhaps even longer."

Heinrici nodded. "It is possible."

"After all," Goebbels prattled on, "imagine how chaotic *our* situation would be if the Führer should suddenly . . ." He stopped himself, realizing where he was heading.

But Hitler gave him a weak smile. "Stalin is really dead. What a wonderful birthday present." He brightened, saw his mistress standing in the doorway on the other side of the room. "Eva!" he called. "Did you hear? My astrologer was correct! He said that good news would come before my birthday."

She smiled prettily.

Hitler suddenly clapped his hands together with something of his old vigor. He turned to Heinrici. "Now we will deal with these mongrel hordes, eh, General? While they are confused and without a leader to give them orders we will drive them from the sacred soil of Germany!"

The expression on Heinrici's face was quite clear to Goebbels. Drive the Russians out of Germany? the general seemed to be saying. With what? We don't have enough troops to defend Berlin, let alone go over to the attack.

But Heinrici said nothing as Hitler marched back to the map and began dictating orders to move army units that may or may not still exist.

Goebbels beamed at his Führer. It's going to be all right, he told himself. Last night he was so gloomy that I thought he was contemplating suicide. But now he is invigorated again. He will pull us through this crisis, just as he's done so often in the past. The astrologer was right; the darkest days have passed. Now we will triumph!

Washington, D.C., April 13 It was mid-morning when the news reached the White House. Roosevelt happened to be meeting with a delegation of farmers from Missouri, led by the Vice President, peppery little Harry Truman.

Grace Tully stepped into the office while the President was in the middle of one his stories about campaigning in the midwest.

"Excuse me, Mr. President. Pardon the interruption, gentlemen, but there is an urgent call from Mr. Stettinius, sir."

Roosevelt's jaunty grin did not fade by a single iota. "The

Secretary of State had better have something very important to say," he told the gaggle of farmers sitting around his broad desk.

"Let's hope he can say it in less than an hour," Truman shot back. "Those people from State seem to take all morning just to say hello!"

The farmers laughed delightedly. Not only were they actually speaking with the President, but they were hearing inside gossip, as well. There would be plenty to tell the folks back home.

Roosevelt's grin evaporated almost the instant he put the phone to his ear. He nodded grimly, said, "Thank you, Edward," then returned the phone to its cradle.

"Gentlemen," he said to the group, "something momentous has happened. Josef Stalin has died."

Silence. No one knew what to say.

Roosevelt continued, "I hope you will excuse me if I cut this visit short. There's a lot that I have to do now."

They all mumbled their understanding and their thanks for his time. Truman shepherded them to the door that led to the corridor. Just before he closed it he said, loud enough for Roosevelt to hear, "Well, that's one less Commie in the world."

"Harry!" called the President.

Truman instantly wheeled about, his face going red.

"Harry, would you be good enough to inform Sam Rayburn and the committee chairmen of this?"

"Yessir, Mr. President. Certainly."

"Thank you."

"They'll all want to see you, you know."

"Yes, of course. Later this afternoon, I suppose. Set up a meeting with Missy, will you."

"Yes, of course." The Vice President closed the door softly.

Roosevelt leaned back in his wheelchair. His secretary was still standing at the doorway to her office.

"Call Henry Stimson for me, will you please? I want him to bring General Marshall here at once. And get Ike's headquarters on the phone and find out if they've heard the news."

She nodded and stepped back into her own office. Alone for a few moments, Roosevelt thought, Uncle Joe has died. That's unexpected. It could mean a lot of changes. A lot of changes.

He reached across the desk and flicked on his intercom. "Get Harry Hopkins in here, too, would you? He's got to go to Moscow to see what the new line-up there will be like."

Kustrin, April 13 "Dead? He's dead?"

The news hit Marshal Zhukov like a thunderbolt. The Man of Steel dead. It was unthinkable. Yet undoubtedly true.

"There's more," said Colonel Novikov.

The two men were walking through the stubble of what had once been an orchard, just outside the German town of Kustrin, on the bank of the River Oder. They spoke quietly together, a hundred meters from the nearest listening ear. Their uniforms were stained with mud and dust, the working clothes of military men in the midst of a ceaseless, grinding campaign.

The trees of the orchard had been shattered to splinters, their stumps blasted, the ground scorched. A blackened burned-out Tiger tank hulked nearby, one tread splayed along the ground like a metallic snake. All that remained of the stone farmhouse was a scattering of smoking rubble. Shell craters pockmarked the ground and the stench of death still hung in the air, a week after the last decaying body had been buried. This was the site of a minor skirmish between the advancing Soviet armies and the stubbornly retreating Germans. The battle here had taken no more than a single springtime afternoon. A few kilometers away, the town of Kustrin itself no longer existed as anything more than a splotch on a map. The buildings had been leveled, the inhabitants who had not been killed had fled westward, away from the advancing Russians.

"More?" Zhukov asked curtly.

Novikov was the intelligence officer on his staff, the son of a man Zhukov had known from cadet days. The father had been killed in Stalin's purges before the war; Zhukov had been able to protect the youngster, but just barely. Now, after nearly four years of continuous fighting, young Novikov looked as gray and worn as his father had.

"Beria was shot," said the colonel. "An army unit surrounded his apartment building last night shortly after the Great One died and one of the officers shot him right there in his own living room."

Zhukov whistled with astonishment. That must have been Khrushchev's work. Cutting off the head of the MGB's private army. Making certain the Red Army won't have to battle the political police. Good for Nikita! He knows when to act. I didn't realize he had the guts for it.

"None of this has been told to the people yet," Novikov went on. "Moscow radio will announce later today that Stalin has been taken ill. By tonight they will say that his illness is very grave. They haven't decided how long to let it go before they announce his death."

"Break the news to the people carefully," Zhukov said. "Yes, that's the right way to go about it. No sense putting them into a panic. Let them get accustomed to the idea that their great leader will no longer be with them."

If Novikov recognized the irony in the marshal's tone he

gave no sign of it. "The story about Beria will be decided upon later, from what I hear."

"Who will take the task of supreme commander of the armies?" Zhukov asked.

The colonel shrugged. "No one knows."

Zhukov turned his eyes toward the west, where the sun was setting fire-red and glowering against the crest of a ridge that had been denuded by artillery fire.

"Who takes Berlin?" Zhukov asked. "Do we do it, or Koniev?" He almost spat the last word.

The colonel shrugged again and repeated, "No one knows."

"It mustn't be Koniev. Whatever happens, we must get to Berlin before he does."

17

London, 14 April   Deep below 10 Downing Street, the underground cabinet room was silent and empty
except for two men. Winston Churchill sat at the center of
the long, green baize-covered table, puffing thoughtfully on
an enormous black cigar. His chair was pushed sideways to
face Anthony Eden, sitting beside him. Eden looked tired,
Churchill thought. No, more than tired. Worse than tired.
He looked weighted with guilt.

"It's been done, then," said Churchill.

Eden nodded somberly. "Apparently they've shot Beria
straight off. They will announce a central committee of
four: Malenkov, Bulganin, Khrushchev and Molotov."

"I know Molotov. An utterly humorless man." Churchill
drew hard on the cigar, making its tip glow bright red in the
dimly lit chamber. He blew a cloud of thick gray smoke
toward the criss-cross beams of the low ceiling.

"The rest?" Eden asked.

"Nonentities, as far as I am concerned. Do you have files on them?"

"Yes, of course. Rather sketchy, I'm afraid."

"We'll have to dig out more information, then."

"Yes."

Churchill studied the younger man's handsome face for a silent moment. "Do you believe that they suspected Beria was in on it?"

With a slight shake of his head, Eden replied, "No, there's no indication that they know anything at all about Broadsword. They simply shot the man to get him out of their way. I suppose, in their way of thinking, it was better than risking a civil war."

Churchill pulled on the cigar again. "I must speak with the President."

"Yes."

The Prime Minister picked up the phone on the table in front of him and ordered a call to Washington. "This changes everything," he said as he replaced the phone on its cradle.

"I understand."

Taking the cigar from his lips, Churchill said, "We had to do it, you know. It makes no sense to win the war against Hitler only to face an intransigent Stalin who's taken half of Europe into his tyrannical clutches."

"I realize that, Winston," said Eden unhappily. "It's only that . . ."

"That what?"

"If this should ever leak out."

"That we assassinated a tyrant? History would hail us as heroes."

"What would the Russians do?"

Churchill thought a moment. Then, "The new leadership would secretly congratulate us, I think."

"And then there's the man who actually did the deed. The radiation must have effected him too. Is he dead, or do they have him in custody? Was he able to do the job without compromising the entire plan, or does the Kremlin already know that we murdered Stalin?"

"There's no indication that they know, you said."

Eden shook his head. "No. Not yet, at least."

"Nor will there be, I'm sure. And if they suspect anything, they will blame it on Beria, whom they've already silenced."

"It's so frightfully risky, Winston."

"It is my risk," Churchill said, his voice rumbling deep in his chest. "Broadsword was my plan. I took the full responsibility. If it is exposed, I will accept the blame." Then he smiled impishly. "Or the credit."

The telephone in front of him buzzed once. "That would be the President."

"Yes."

Eden started to push his chair back, but Churchill motioned for him to stay as he picked up the phone.

The voice in the phone said through crackling static, "One moment for the President, Mr. Prime Minister."

Looking into Eden's troubled eyes, Churchill thought how odd it was that men could send millions into battle and accept with perfect ease the slaughter of ten thousand of the enemy, yet feel so queasy at the death of one man. Secretly, he felt some pangs of remorse himself. He had known Stalin for nearly four years. The man was a tyrant, a beast, as bad as Hitler for certain. Yet Churchill had eaten and drunk with him. And coldly had him murdered.

"Winston?" came Roosevelt's voice.

Churchill visibly brightened. He smiled as he said into the phone, "Franklin, have you heard the news?"

Washington, D.C., April 14   Roosevelt was sitting at his desk in the Oval Office, golden afternoon sunshine lighting the tall windows behind him.

"Yes, Winston, I agree," he was saying into the phone. "This changes everything. I have already spoken with our ambassador in Moscow. Harry Hopkins is on his way to meet the new leaders, and I will speak with Molotov later today. As I understand it, things are in a considerable turmoil over there."

General Marshall watched the President's face and waited to hear the word "Berlin." He knew Churchill would bring it up again.

Beside Marshall sat Henry Stimson, the Secretary of War. A gentleman from the old school, lean, reserved, almost seventy-seven years old, Stimson had served every president since Woodrow Wilson. He was a Republican, and he could be flinty at times. But he had Roosevelt's absolute trust, and Marshall's unreserved admiration.

The third man facing the desk was Bill Donovan, looking more like a Wall Street lawyer—which he had been—than the head of the intelligence organization, the innocuously named Office of Strategic Services. He puffed nervously on a cigarette as Roosevelt chatted with Churchill.

Finally, "I'll call you later this evening, Winston, about that. We have a lot of thinking to do, and we have to do it quickly. . . . Yes, I agree. . . . Yes. If we can, I think we should, yes. . . . Very well, Winston. I'll ring you back about midnight, your time. . . . Good. Until then."

The three men waited expectantly as the President put the phone down.

Roosevelt was silent for a moment, then he asked Donovan, "Bill, what's going on inside the Kremlin now?"

"Hard to tell, Mr. President."

"The Russian armies have stopped their advances," General Marshall volunteered. "That may be for resupply, before they launch their assault on Berlin. Or it may be for political reasons. We can't tell."

"Henry," the President turned to Stimson, "if you were sitting behind this desk, what would you do?"

Stimson, dressed as usual in a dark three-piece suit with his Phi Beta Kappa key on a gold chain, looked up at the ceiling, as if for inspiration. "I would move ahead just as planned. I would wait to see some indication from the Russians as to how this sudden change in leadership is going to effect them."

"There is one thing that we ought to keep in mind," Donovan said. "Goering is willing to surrender all the German forces on the western and Italian fronts."

"So that they can be moved against the Russians," Marshall added, his voice crisp with disdain.

"Winston still wants us to take Berlin," said the President.

The three men fell silent.

"Could we do it?" Roosevelt asked.

"I don't think there's much fight left in the German armies facing us," Donovan said.

"There is bound to be some confusion among the Russians," said Stimson. "At least for the next few days. Perhaps longer. There may be a power struggle in the Kremlin. I understand they have already liquidated Beria."

"General Marshall," asked the President, "what do you say?"

A thousand thoughts raced through Marshall's mind. He saw the coffins and the rows of crosses in military cemeteries all across Europe. He saw Churchill glowing in the light of conquest, cigar in one hand and the other lifted in his V-for-Victory sign. But he also saw American soldiers marching down Unter den Linden, past the Brandenberg Gate, triumphant for all the world to see.

"Sir," said the general, his mind made up, "I still regard Berlin as a political prize that is not worth the casualties it would cost to take it. But if you decide that it should be taken, then I ask only one thing."

"Yes, General?" Roosevelt was starting to smile.

"That we don't hand this plum to Montgomery and the British. If you're going to order Ike to take Berlin, then it has to be an *American* army that takes it."

"My thinking exactly," said the President, his smile beaming radiantly. "That is what I'll tell the Prime Minister this evening. If he wants Berlin, he's got to allow us to take it."

18

Buchenwald, 15 April   Stalin's death made scant difference to the men of the U.S. Third Army. But their capture of the German town of Buchenwald did. You could smell the nearby camp from the town. The strong springtime breeze carried the stench of burnt flesh on it.

General Patton was sitting in the right-hand seat of the jeep as it jounced along the paved road toward the camp. His sergeant driver kept his eyes straight ahead. Major Leslie, commander of the unit that had stumbled onto the death camp the previous day, sat in the back, his long legs crammed in so that his knees were almost touching his lantern jaw.

Patton twisted around and yelled over the noise of the jeep's engine, "The people in the town claim they didn't know anything about this camp?"

"Yessir," said Leslie, his face grim. "I spoke with the burgomeister and several members of the town council.

They all told me that the camp was off-limits and they had no idea of what was going on there."

Patton grumbled something unintelligible. His face had a pinched, nervous look to it.

The smell was getting worse. Overhead the sky was an innocent clear blue. The ground around the road seemed untouched by war. The German troops had retreated here without much of a fight; there was hardly a shell crater to be seen. Farmhouses looked intact. There were even a couple of scrawny cows grazing on the new grass out there.

"Gates coming up, sir," said the driver. Patton nodded.

A full squad of GIs was in front of the main gate of the tall barbed-wire fence. They snapped to attention and shouldered their guns as the jeep rolled past them. Patton scowled at the sign over the gate; he knew enough German to translate, "Freedom through work."

The general saw his first prisoners as the jeep rolled to a stop just inside the gate. Human scarecrows in filthy, lice-ridden striped pajamas, their emaciated limbs barely able to hold them up, their faces hollow and gaunt with starvation and enduring agony. Their eyes had the expression that GIs called "the thousand-yard stare": unfocused, unwilling to see the horror that had engulfed them. They had not the strength to celebrate their liberation; happiness was an emotion that had long since been beaten out of them. They simply stood to one side of the gate and stared like accusing ghosts.

Patton stared back at them. "My sweet Christ," he muttered as he climbed out of the jeep. "My sweet Jesus Christ."

"Those are the ones strong enough to stand," said Major Leslie.

The major led the tour. Barracks where the living dead lay stacked in makeshift bunks five high; those in the top bunks too weak to get down. "So far we've found about half of them already dead from starvation," Leslie explained. Rooms that Patton at first thought were public showers. Leslie explained they were gas chambers; the prisoners were herded inside after being stripped, then the "water faucets" streamed cyanide gas. After any gold in their teeth was pried out they were carried by the cartload to the ovens. Patton scowled at the ovens, huge commercial bakery ovens, and told one of the officers accompanying him to make a note of the manufacturer's name engraved clearly on the doors.

Then they went outside to the mass graves, where bodies had been bulldozed by the hundreds into open pits to get them hidden before the advancing Americans could discover what had gone on here. "They had too many corpses to burn," said Leslie in a flat, strained voice. "The ovens couldn't keep up with the killings."

Patton stared into a half-covered pit, stared at the naked, dirt-encrusted bodies of men and women and little girls and babies, their mouths open in screams, their eyes wide and pleading.

His guts churned. Suddenly the general wheeled and ran off several paces, vomiting like a green soldier who had seen his first dead body.

The officers milled around nervously, not knowing what to do for their general. A corporal ran over to Patton with a white handkerchief in his hand.

"It got me the same way, sir, first time I saw it," the corporal said. Patton took the handkerchief and wiped his mouth, his eyes scanning the kid's face. No more then nineteen or twenty years old.

"God help me, son," he muttered. "I've seen battle and I've led men to their deaths, but I've never seen anything like this."

The corporal nodded sympathetically. "There ain't nothing like this to see, sir. Except maybe the other camps these bastards set up."

Patton pulled himself together and strode back to his waiting officers. "I want pictures of all this. All of it! Movie pictures. The whole world's got to see what vermin these Krauts are. The whole goddamned *world!.*"

"Yessir."

He wheeled on Major Leslie. "And you get that goddamned burgomeister and his town council down here. I want them to get a good look at this. Get the whole damned town to look! Make 'em see it!"

"Yes, sir," said the major.

Patton started back toward his jeep. "They didn't know what was going on, did they? I'll bet not one of them was a fucking Nazi, either.'

Paris, 16 April   "George, you shouldn't have come here," said General Eisenhower.

The raging fury that Patton had felt the previous day at Buchenwald had burned away. Now, at SHAEF headquarters in this luxurious Parisian hotel it had been replaced by a searing urgency: hatred had turned into zeal, anger at the Germans into impatience with his own commander.

Ike was standing beside his desk, an ornate French creation with frail little legs and baroque decorations carved into its bleached wood. In his waist-length combat jacket and comfortable slacks he seemed almost unmilitary compared against the bristling figure of George Patton, pistols on his hips, boots polished to a mirror shine, rows of ribbons adorning his chest.

General Omar Bradley sat on one of the funny little French chairs set against the wall between the long windows, his pipestem legs stretched out like a pair of soda straws. The hotel room had a high, coffered ceiling, exquisitely detailed drapes and wallpaper, and lovely fragile-looking furniture. But its floor was bare. Some retreating Nazi officer had rolled up the rug and carted it back to Germany with him.

Patton's gleaming helmet rested on the desk beside Eisenhower. "Ike, I'm trying to help you. I'll make you President of the United States with this!"

Eisenhower's patience was at the breaking point. Not only had Washington countermanded his decision to leave Berlin to the Russians, but now George was here hot and steaming to lead the charge to the German capital.

Instead of replying to his old friend, Eisenhower turned his back on Patton and went over to the window. It was raining out there, not much to see. Patton suddenly felt as gray and chilled as the weather.

"George," Bradley said, slowly getting up from his chair, "you can see how impractical it would be . . ."

"I can get Berlin for you!" Patton insisted, his thin voice flaring high, almost girlish. "I want to get my hands on that bastard Hitler. After what I saw a couple of days ago, I want to personally kick his balls off!"

Bradley looked like a tired schoolteacher: high forehead, face creased from decisions, round little wire-rimmed glasses. He just shook his head, the expression on his face half amused, half disgusted.

"You think Simpson or Hodges can do it, Brad? Hell, Simpson just *retreated* back across the goddamned Elbe! Retreated!"

Eisenhower turned to face Patton, his composure somewhat restored. "George, Simpson's advanced guard retreated because they were out of fuel and ammunition. You know that. As soon as they're resupplied they'll move forward again."

Bradley put a hand on Patton's shoulder. "George, if we had been planning to punch through to Berlin from the beginning, you would have been placed in the center of the drive. You know that. But until two days ago it was decided to leave Berlin to the Russians. As things stand now your Third Army is too far south for the drive to Berlin."

"The hell it is!" Patton snapped. "Brad, you remember in Tunisia when I moved the whole damned II Corps for the assault on Bizerte? Turned a hundred thousand men and their supporting units around behind that limey Alexander's rear in two days. Remember?"

Bradley grinned. "Yeah, I remember."

"And Bastogne?" Patton's eyes moved to Eisenhower. "Turned the whole Third Army ninety degrees and relieved Bastogne. Through the snow and fog."

Eisenhower said nothing. But he knew that Patton was calling in the due bills that he owed him.

"Let me show you how I can do this," Patton said, unbuttoning the flap of his tunic pocket. He pulled out a square of paper, unfolded it and spread it across the rickety-looking desk. Bradley and Eisenhower saw that it was a map.

"Now here's where my Third Army is, in the south. I can pivot my men on this axis here, swing behind Hodge's First Army and come out punching right here, between Dessau and Magdeburg. That's less than a hundred twenty kilometers from Berlin. Whatever old Adolph's got in that area won't be expecting the whole weight of the Third Army against them. They'll crack wide open and I'll get to Berlin before the Russians even know we're coming. It'll be like the dash across France, all over again!"

Bradley shook his head in a mixture of admiration and exasperation. "I've got to admit, George, if anybody could do it, you could."

Eisenhower snorted with ill-concealed discontent. "It makes a stew out of all our plans. The logistics . . ." He frowned. But kept on studying the map.

"Ike, you know Hodges can't make that kind of a breakthrough. What would you prefer, letting *Montgomery* try it? It'd take him a fucking month just to get his tea things ready!"

Despite himself, Eisenhower grinned.

Bradley added, "If we can punch through the way George wants to, the casualties might not be so bad."

"The Krauts don't want to fight us," Patton said. "They'll fold up and quit."

"There was talk of Goering arranging a truce," Eisenhower said.

Patton's nostrils twitched. "Wait till you see Buchenwald, Ike. We can't make a truce with these murdering sonsofbitches."

Eisenhower gave one of his snorting sighs. "It's the logistics that worries me. Keeping your lead elements from bogging down means supplying them with fuel and ammo . . ."

"We'll start the Red Ball Express again," Patton said eagerly. "Get those truckdrivers on the road again, just like in France."

"It worked in France," Bradley admitted.

"Not all the way to the Rhine, though," said Eisenhower.

"Come on, Ike! It's only a lousy hundred twenty kilometers. You'll be leading the parade down Unter den Linden before the month is out! They'll elect you President for this!"

Eisenhower's face flushed slightly. He bent over the map and asked, "What do you think of having airborne troops dropped in advance of your lead elements?"

19

Berlin, 16 April   "I absolutely forbid it!" Hitler shouted.

"But my Führer," pleaded Goering.

"Surrender? Never! Not to the mongrel Americans and certainly not to that fat monster Churchill."

Goering did not even wince at the word "fat." He was too concerned with winning Hitler to his plan.

"It's not a surrender, not really," he said. "We negotiate a truce and move our armies to face the Russians."

"No!" Hitler shouted, so loud that his voice rang echoes off the concrete walls.

"But my Führer . . ."

Hitler stared at his Reichsmarschall with a mixture of fury and loathing in his gray eyes. He had received Goering in the cramped little room he used as a study, deep in the bunker that Goering more and more thought of as a crypt. The final resting place for all the dreams of a greater Germany.

Hitler strode to the door, abruptly turned and said in a milder voice, "Sit down, Goering. Sit. We should not raise our voices to one another; it's bad for the morale of the others."

Goering took one of the overstuffed chairs, thinking that only one of them had raised his voice. Hitler sat opposite him, on his favorite armchair.

"The Americans and British cannot be trusted to abide by a truce," Hitler said. "Once our armies are withdrawn to the east, they will march in and occupy as much of the Fatherland as they can."

Goering wanted to say that he did not agree, but he kept silent.

"The Russians, on the other hand," Hitler went on, "are in a state of confusion. Their advance has stopped. And we know that their two leading generals, Koniev and Zhukov, hate each other."

Goering nodded glumly.

"History goes in cycles, my dear Goering. In cycles. We are now at a turning point. In Frederick the Great's time, Prussia was surrounded by enemies and on the verge of annihilation. But the tsarina died and the coalition against Prussia fell apart. In Nineteen Seventeen Russia collapsed in the Bolshevik Revolution. I tell you that Russia will collapse again, now. With Stalin dead, the people will revolt against their Bolshevik government. I know they will. All we have to do is wait for it to happen."

"But while we wait, brave men are dying needlessly," Goering found the courage to say.

"It is not needless if they protect the Fatherland from the invaders!"

Goering admitted it with a shrug.

"Nor will we passively wait for events to sort themselves out," Hitler said. "In the west, we will remain on the defensive. Eisenhower shows no great will to push us hard. He is a political general, not a fighting general."

"But there is Patton . . ."

"He is being diverted to the south, to find the redoubt that the Americans believe we have prepared in the Bavarian mountains."

Goering did wince this time. He had promised his Führer an impregnable fortress in those wooded mountains. Not much more than a few dugouts had actually been built.

"In the east," Hitler went on, his eyes glowing brighter, "we face a situation similar to Tannenberg, in the First War. Two Russian armies invading the Fatherland, led by generals who hate each other. Just as Hindenburg did then, I will drive a wedge between the two Russian armies and then defeat each one in turn!"

As mildly as he could, Goering asked, "Do you have the resources to accomplish this, my Führer?"

"Reinforcements are streaming toward Berlin! That is why we remain on the defensive in the west. I am stripping the units there of every man they can spare."

"But wouldn't it be better if we got the Americans and British to agree to a truce on the western front? Then we could—"

"They will not agree to a truce!" Hitler snapped. "I know this. They will insist on unconditional surrender. They will not be moved from their alliance with the Russians. They are too stupid and too stubborn to see that it is the Russians who threaten civilization. Churchill and that Jew Roosevelt are in league with the communists! Can't you see that?"

Goering could see that his Führer's mind was made up, and that arguing would be pointless. But he sat there for another two hours as Hitler worked himself into a spluttering, storming rage, railing against the archfiend Churchill and the cripple Roosevelt who was secretly a Jew.

Finally the furor died away and Hitler's face went from angry red to the dead-gray color that this underground life had caused. Goering recognized anew how his Führer had been living out of the sun for years now; it was not merely this recent descent into the bunker that had given him this prison pallor. For years Hitler had spent his days and nights in conference chambers and map rooms, behind thick concrete walls or deep underground in his various headquarters.

"You may go, Goering," the Führer was saying. "I know you want to be in your beloved Carinhall."

Goering blinked. The Russians had overrun his mansion north of the city more than a week ago. He had personally supervised the dynamiting of the house and all the other buildings, even his first wife's mausoleum.

As he got up from the chair, Goering said, "Come with me, Führer. To Bavaria. You can conduct the battle from there."

Slowly, painfully, Hitler struggled to his feet. "No, I will remain here in Berlin. We will win, Goering! You'll see. We'll drive the Russians back to their steppes."

"We could be better assured of that if we could withdraw the forces facing the Americans and British," Goering suggested one more time.

Hitler shook his head wearily. "No, they will never agree to such a truce."

"Let me negotiate with them," Goering pleaded. "Perhaps—"

"It's the camps," Hitler said, his voice sinking to a whisper. "They've found some of the camps. They will never negotiate with us now. The Jews have destroyed us."

Goering's heart fell. Belsen. Buchenwald. Dachau. Auschwitz. The Führer is right. The Americans will never negotiate with us once they see the camps. Our last hope is gone.

20

Frankfurt, 16 April   First squad, third platoon, I company,
506th Parachute Regiment, 101st Airborne Division, jounced and rattled through the bombed-out remains of Frankfurt as part of a long convoy of trucks and jeeps.

The sun had set, and the twilight was deepening into darkness. As long as the light lasted, Jarvick stared at the wreckage that the bombers had inflicted. As far as he could see, not a house or a building stood intact. Walls gone, roofs blown away, windows staring mute and empty. Only this one street had been cleared away by the Army Engineers' bulldozers to make an avenue leading to the front.

What was it Hemingway had said about this kind of thing? Jarvick searched his memory. From the First World War, from *A Farewell to Arms.* "The sudden interior of a house." Something like that. He saw a three-story house, front wall gone, bathtub hanging perilously from the crumbling remains of the second-story flooring. Sudden interior. Hemingway knows how to use words.

Jarvick would not let his buddies know of his reverence for literature. They kidded him enough about being a former newspaper reporter who was just as much in the dark about where they were going as any hillbilly recruit. Hollis thought he was too serious; called him an ant. My own fault, Jarvick thought. I started it by calling him a grasshopper.

He thought about his wife, who had taken over his job as news editor back at the paper in Turnersville. Was she lonely? Jarvick ached for her. Despite the occasional opportunity he had been faithful to her, except for that drunken spree after the Third Army broke through the Germans and saved their asses at Bastogne. That had been a wild couple of nights; the Belgian and the French women had been more than willing and there was no force on Earth that could stop men who had faced death a scant thousand yards away.

Was his wife being faithful? Sure she was. It's been thirty-two months since I've seen her. Jarvick knew the time down to the day: thirty-two months, three weeks, six days. Sure she's been faithful. She wouldn't screw around with another guy. She's not the type.

He did a little multiplication in his head. Nine hundred eighty-seven days. And nights. Almost a thousand. Then a thousand and one, like the Arabian Nights.

On through the night the trucks kept rolling, far beyond Frankfurt, heading east, toward the fighting. Jarvick and the others sat as numb as animals being hauled cross-country by a circus. They drowsed, heads bobbing as they slumped on chests. Snores and grunts competed with the hypnotic drone of the truck engines and the whine of tires on pavement.

Only Jarvick remained awake. His rifle clamped between his knees, he leaned his head back until his helmet was pillowed against the truck's taut fabric top. He had parachuted into Normandy in the dark almost a year ago. He had survived D day and the breakout from the beachhead. Then the bloody shambles at Eindhoven last September. He had survived Bastogne and the Battle of the Bulge. Without a scratch. Half the platoon killed or wounded so badly they never came back, but he had not even been nicked. Don't let me be killed now, he prayed to no one in particular. Let me be shot clean, in the leg or shoulder or somewhere they can fix. Just let it be bad enough to get me back to the States.

But he felt certain that he would not get through the next battle, wherever it was going to be. He knew that for sure.

Kaluga, 17 April It was not much of a town, thought Grigori Gagarin, although fortunately the fighting here had been comparatively light. Most of the buildings still stood. Only a few were pockmarked by shell fragments or bullet holes.

There was no material for new construction, of course; all available materials were going to the war effort. Still, some of the townspeople had managed to patch up their damaged homes with makeshift repairs. There was not even glass to replace shattered windows, but Grigori saw rough-made wooden shutters, burlap curtains, even scraps of tattered German uniforms where windows had once been. And the city hall, a dull gray brick building, showed splotches of lumber and stone and uneven rows of rough red bricks covering over the damage that had been done during the fighting, more than two years earlier.

Yuri acted as if it were a holy shrine, though, tugging at

his big brother's hand, practically dragging him through the streets from the railroad station toward the little stream that flowed off at the town's outskirts.

Grigori had told the administrator of Yuri's distant school that the lad was needed at home for a family medical emergency. Which was no lie. Grigori knew he was near death; he wanted to see his baby brother one more time before he closed his eyes forever. It had taken all his skill and effort to get Yuri released from school for a week and put onto a train for Moscow. As the private secretary of the deceased Stalin, Grigori still had considerable powers of persuasion among the lower echelons of the state. But those powers were waning as the new commissariat gradually took control of the shocked nation. No matter, thought Grigori. I won't need the power of my former office for more than another few days.

Yuri had surprised Grigori by insisting on a visit to Kaluga. The boy was aflame to see the place. Why not? thought Grigori. It's the last favor I'll be able to do for him. It's the last time I'll see him.

Going on twelve years old, Yuri completely failed to see how sick his brother was. The unconscious indifference of youth. He was so excited at being released from school for a week and the prospect of going to Kaluga that he paid no attention at all to Grigori's condition.

Grigori slept most of the time on the four-hour train ride to Kaluga. He was in constant pain, all his joints ached, and he had difficulty keeping food down. His gums were bloody, as were his bowel movements. His hair was coming out in patches. He was losing weight and his skin had an unhealthy sheen. He felt cold, chilled to the bone, despite the sunny springtime warmth of the day. And despite his chill, he sweated from every pore of his body.

But once the train finally rumbled into Kaluga station, Yuri grabbed his brother's hand and almost ran out to the stream and the little house that he revered as a shrine.

The home of Konstantin Ivanovich Tsiolkovsky.

"I never heard of him," said Grigori as he wearily followed his brother down the dirt path that led to the wood frame house.

"He was a great man!" Yuri exclaimed, his voice high with excitement. "A revolutionary thinker. A pioneer."

Revolutionary? Pioneer? Grigori leaned against the sagging fence that fronted the house. It was nothing more than a cottage, really. There couldn't be more than two or three rooms inside.

"We read about him in school. My instructor told me that one day Tsiolkovsky will be famous all around the world."

"Famous? For what?"

"Space flight!" said Yuri. "Flying to the Moon and Mars. Even to the stars!"

Grigori would have laughed if he had not been in such pain.

Yuri ignored his brother's seeming lack of enthusiasm; he had enough for the two of them. The cottage was kept by an elderly woman who seemed happy to have visitors. She showed the two Gagarin brothers through Tsiolkovsky's study, where Yuri marveled over shabby old notebooks filled with strange drawings of machines that looked like nothing Grigori had ever seen.

"Rockets," explained Yuri, his voice low, subdued, as if he were in a cathedral. Grigori had heard that hushed tone in many men, in the presence of Stalin.

The woman saw that Grigori was near collapse and brought him into the kitchen. It was little more than a shed tacked onto the rear of the cottage. She sat Grigori at the wooden table and gave him a glass of tea. Yuri was still in the study, poring over Tsiolkovsky's open notebooks, hands locked behind his back to ensure his promise not to touch anything.

"He is your brother?" the elderly woman asked. Her hair was gray, her thickset body solid and strong, her face seamed with a lifetime of cares and fears. Yet she survives. Like Mother Russia, Grigori thought. She survives despite everything the world throws at her.

"Yes," he answered. "My only living relative."

"Does he know how sick you are?"

"I have not told him."

"You should, you know. You shouldn't let it come as a shock to him."

"I intended to. He wanted so to visit this place, though, that I didn't have the heart to tell him before we got here."

"He is a bright lad. He will go far. Not many realize what an important man my uncle was."

"He was your uncle?" The woman faded out of focus slightly and then back in. Grigori felt faint.

She nodded. "He was a teacher of mathematics. But he dreamed great dreams."

"Apparently Yuri shares those dreams," Grigori managed to say.

"That is good."

He could hardly speak, he felt so exhausted. The woman made a bowl of hot borscht for him, with a steaming potato in it.

"For strength," she said.

Grigori thanked her weakly and spooned up a little of it. After a while he realized that the sun was setting. Feeling somewhat stronger, he struggled to his feet and pulled a few crumpled ruble notes from his pocket.

"It is not allowed, comrade," said the woman firmly.

"To repay you for the borscht and tea."

She hesitated a moment, then took one bill from his hand. "You are a kind man."

"Thank you."

Grigori tottered back into the darkening study and pulled a reluctant Yuri away from the wooden models of airplanes and space ships that he was admiring, hands still clasped tightly behind his back.

It took all Grigori's remaining strength to walk slowly through the twilight back to the railroad station. They waited in silence for the train back to Moscow, Grigori simply trying to keep his heart pumping, Yuri lost in dreams about adventures in space.

At last the train chuffed in and they boarded it. A vendor plied through the car's aisle, offering snacks and drinks. Grigori was too exhausted to eat, but Yuri feasted on thick slabs of dark bread and hot tea.

As the train hurtled through the night, wheels clicking on the tracks, Grigori watched his little brother. He was a handsome lad, with winning ways. And intelligent, too, you could see that in his clear blue eyes.

"Do you really think," he asked, "that people will fly to the Moon some day?"

Yuri practically bounced up and down on their seat, he nodded so enthusiastically. "Yes! Of course! I want to be one of them."

"You do?"

"Yes. To fly into space. To go to the Moon. Or maybe to Mars. That's what I want to do when I grow up."

Grigori smiled faintly. "I thought you wanted to be an aviator and shoot down the enemies of the State."

"Oh, the war's almost over, Grisha. And flying into space will be much more fun than shooting at people."

"That's right," Grigori said, feeling an immense relief flow into his soul. "That's true."

"I'll have to learn to fly airplanes first, I suppose," Yuri went on. "But then I'll learn to fly rockets. You'll see!"

Shaking his had gently, Grigori said, "No, little Yuri, I'm afraid I won't live to see you fly a rocket."

Yuri's eyes went wide. "What do you mean?"

"I am dying, Yuri. I have a few days more, at most."

"Dying?" Yuri stared at his brother, seeing him truly for the first time. "Dying?" he repeated, in a whisper.

Grigori nodded. "I have made all the necessary arrangements for you. You will receive my pension. You are already registered in Moscow University. Everything is set—"

"But you can't die!" Yuri said desperately. "You're my brother! I love you!"

With his remaining strength Grigori pulled Yuri to him and held his head against his breast. "I love you, too, little Yuri. More than life itself, I love you. But I must die. I must. It will be hard for you, I know, with no one to look after you. But you are strong and brave and intelligent. You will be successful in life in anything you want to do. The world will be a better place for you, Yuri. The war will be over. A new world can be built. You can even fly into space if you truly want to. I did it all for you, Yuri. I give you this new world as my final gift . . ."

The breath left his body. Grigori Gagarin died there in the railroad car with his arms clasped around his sobbing brother, a final smile of peace on his bloodless lips.

21

Moscow, 18 April Molotov's office was thick with smoke. It was a spacious corner room in the Presidium building, with a pretty view of St. Basil's ornate colorful spires and the Moscow River. But both the foreign minister and his visitor were chain smokers; the office windows were shut against the cold blustering wind outside, and the air inside the office was a murky gray haze.

Which did not bother Viachislav M. Molotov in the slightest; nor his visitor, Harry Hopkins. They sat in comfortable leather armchairs by one of the closed windows, heads bent together in earnest discussion.

Molotov was a tiny man, with small delicate hands and a little black moustache that made Hopkins want to laugh. But the Russian's face was usually set in a dour scowl of disapproval. It was a roundish face, pinched in the middle by a pince-nez. His dark hair was receding, but not a touch of gray was evident.

Hopkins was not much bigger than the foreign minister. He wore a gray suit, wrinkled from his long trip. His face had an ash-gray pallor to it. He had been an aide and confident to Franklin Roosevelt since before his presidency, when FDR had been governor of New York. Hopkins had held a variety of positions in Albany and Washington; their titles never worried him, for he was always interested in actual power rather than its trappings. As long as he was close enough to guide his chief, he was satisfied.

". . . so you see," Molotov was saying, "that despite Stalin's unexpected death, we will continue to prosecute the war against the Nazis. The Soviet Union will not change its goals; our armies in the field will keep on bearing the brunt of the battle."

Hopkins, caught in the act of lighting a fresh cigarette on the stub his last one, coughed a bit and replied, "Are you implying that our troops aren't fighting as hard?"

Molotov's iron expression did not change in the slightest. "I am merely reflecting on the fact that Hitler has always put his best forces against us. Your troops have had a comparatively easy time of it."

Hopkins puffed his new cigarette into a fierce glow, thinking, He's not going to give you a better opportunity than this.

"All right," he said, making himself smile, "I will tell the President that we should move faster and harder against the Germans. Instead of stopping at the Elbe, we'll push on as hard as we can to give your armies as much help as possible."

Molotov blinked behind his pince-nez once, twice. "That could cause some confusion to our plans."

"Which plans?"

"The occupation zones were clearly delineated at the Yalta conference."

"The occupation zones," Hopkins answered smoothly, "are for the occupation of Germany and Austria after the fighting stops. What we're talking about now is the actual fighting. We intend to give you all the help we can."

"But General Eisenhower's communication of twenty-eighth March said that your forces would stop at the Elbe."

Hopkins waved a hand in the air. "That will be changed immediately. We don't want your troops facing the Nazis without all the help we can provide. We're allies, after all."

Molotov's suspicious scowl deepened into a thoughtful frown. "The purpose of stopping at the Elbe was to make certain that our armies do not accidentally fire upon one another."

"I'm sure the generals in the field can work out recognition signals and such."

The Russian foreign minister sank back in his chair. "It would be a pity if our troops killed one another by accident."

Hopkins shrugged. "This is war. Even if a few minor accidents do happen, there will be far fewer of your men lost that way than if you had to slug it out with the Germans by yourselves. No, we *must* give you all the help we can. History would never forgive us if we didn't, and the American people wouldn't forgive us, either. They greatly admire the way you've fought off the Nazi invaders."

It was Molotov's turn to start a new cigarette. He opened the lacquered box on the sherry table between their two chairs and saw that it was almost empty. It had been full when this conversation had started, several hours ago.

Hopkins leaned forward with his Zippo lighter and flicked it into flame. Molotov drew deeply, then exhaled smoke through his nose.

"We have heard rumors," he said, shifting the subject, "that Goering is seeking a truce on the western front."

"Oh?" Hopkins replied innocently.

"He wants to shift the troops facing your armies to the east, to face ours. The same for the German troops in Italy," said Molotov.

Hopkins shook his head. "I've heard nothing about that, and if I had I would have advised the President against it. Our policy is firm: unconditional surrender and no separate deals."

Both Hopkins and Molotov knew that the Soviet foreign minister had quietly opened negotiations with the German foreign minister, Ribbentrop, in 1943, seeking a separate truce.

"You are firm on that?" Molotov asked.

"Unconditional surrender," Hopkins repeated. "No truce, no separate peace."

Molotov puffed on his cigarette for a few silent moments. Then, "I have arranged for Khrushchev and Malenkov to have supper with us tonight."

"Fine," said Hopkins. "I'd be delighted to meet them. But isn't Bulganin going to join us?"

Molotov almost smiled. "Comrade Bulganin is in the Caucasus region, supervising new oil-well installations."

"I see," said Hopkins, thinking, Bulganin is already being used as an errand boy. The big three are Molotov, Khrushchev and Malenkov.

He reported as much by coded radio message to Washington that night from his quarters in the American embassy, after a long and vodka-soaked supper in the Kremlin. Hopkins also added that he had told his hosts that the U.S. and British armies would not stop at the Elbe River.

"I did not mention Berlin per se," he reported, "but I left the implication clear."

Molotov did mention Berlin to Khrushchev that night,

after Hopkins left. "They mean to seize Berlin," he said. "I am certain of it."

Khrushchev, who had behaved quite drunkenly during the long supper, looked at the foreign minister with narrowed eyes. "Then we must order Zhukov and Koniev to take the city before the Americans can."

"But which one? Zhukov or Koniev?"

"Both of them!" snapped Khrushchev. "Let them both strive for the prize."

Berne, 19 April General Wolff was wearing the same light brown three-piece suit as he paced slowly down the street alongside Allen Dulles. The American head of OSS operations in Europe puffed on his pipe, still looking like a visiting college professor.

"If it were not so tragic it would be funny," Wolff was saying as they walked past a row of little shops in the warm afternoon sunlight.

"So what's Goering going to do?" Dulles asked. They were speaking in English, and kept their voices low despite the fact that there was no one to eavesdrop on them except a few elderly women out shopping.

"After Goering left Berlin, Himmler convinced Hitler that the Reichsmarschall was going to make his own surrender to the Allies. Hitler went into a tantrum and revoked the order of Nineteen Forty-one that made Goering his political heir. Himmler then gave orders to Bormann to arrest the Reichsmarschall. Bormann sent a squad of SS men to Burg Valdenstein with the threat of death if they did not follow their orders and arrest Goering."

"My Lord!"

Wolff chuckled uneasily. "But *Der Dicke* outfoxed them, as usual. His castle was already occupied by a battalion of

Luftwaffe troops. Goering placed the SS men under his own 'protective custody!' "

"Can he get away with that?"

"If your troops move in quickly enough, he can. He is sitting in his castle, waiting to surrender to you. He has decided that continued fighting is hopeless."

Dulles took the pipe from his teeth. "I'll get a message to SHAEF right away. Our boys ought to be able to take that area in a day or two."

"I would have thought they would already have advanced that far, but apparently they stopped some days ago. Your front lines have not advanced in several days."

Dulles said nothing, but thought, For the chance to capture Hermann Goering, Ike can push the men along a bit, I'm sure.

"It seems to me," Wolff went on, "as if your armies have stopped their advance all along the western front."

"Logistics," Dulles said. "It's hard to keep the front-line troops supplied when they're advancing so fast."

"Yes," Wolff said slowly, drawing the word out. "Either that, or a repositioning of the armies for a fresh assault."

Dulles swiftly decided that he would not be drawn into that area. "What are you going to do, personally? And Kesselring? Is he still willing to surrender his forces in Italy?"

"We have never said we were willing to surrender!"

Dulles smiled. "No, come to think of it, I guess you didn't. But don't you think it's about time that we discussed the possibility?"

22

Dessau, 20 April Technical Sergeant Kirby Jones hunkered down and sat on the grass, his back against the left front wheel of his deuce-and-a-half. He wiped sweat off his brow. In the past forty-eight hours he and his squad had moved sixteen truckloads of fuel, ammo, food, and lubrication oil over a hundred miles of country roads, winding their way through long columns of clanking growling tanks, self-propelled artillery pieces, tank destroyers, other trucks loaded with troops.

Private Deke Jefferson sank down to the ground beside him. "Okay. I cleaned the sparkplugs and checked th' timing. It's all fine now."

"Better be," muttered Jones.

"Whoo-ee, I'm bushed. I ain't slept since Christmas, feels like."

Jones gave him a lazy smile. "Better get some shut-eye now, man. Once ol' Blood 'n Guts gets them tanks movin' across the river there ain't gonna be any sleep for any of us."

"The voice of experience, huh?" But Jefferson had already pushed his helmet liner over his eyes.

"You wasn't with us last summer. We drove them danged trucks till they fell apart, all the way across France, every day, every night, with ol' Blood 'n Guts hollerin' all the time for us to go faster."

Jefferson's only answer was a gentle snore.

Jones wished he could sleep too. But he had seen something that morning that kept him awake. A black infantry platoon. Whole damned platoon, all black men just like himself. Black noncoms, even black officers.

The draft must be scraping the bottom of the barrel if they're forming combat units out of niggers, he said to himself. Damned white officers don't trust us to fight. Not till now.

He wondered what some of those southern crackers thought about black infantry. He had heard that there was a whole fighter squadron of blacks, but the air force was only a distant dream for the men on the ground and it might have been just a story one nigger told to another to make them both feel better.

Try as he might, Jones could not sleep. Here he was, twenty-four years old, going on fifty. He had been in the army for three years now. He had been shelled by Kraut artillery and twice he had been strafed by the few German planes still in the sky. But he was only a truck driver, not a combat soldier. He wondered what it would be like. Could I kill another man? he asked himself. Guess so, if I had to. If he was one of those motherfucking Nazis who says they gonna get rid of all the black people, I'd kill the sonofabitch all right.

Three years in the army had taught him to be grateful

that he was not on the front line, not a combat soldier. But he couldn't help feeling disappointed that nobody in the whole entire U.S. Army considered him fit to be trusted with actual fighting. And he felt even more disappointed with himself that he was inwardly kind of glad that he didn't have to go into the line where he might get himself killed.

He finally drowsed off in the early morning sun, only to be awakened by the thundering roar of artillery. He jumped to his feet, Jefferson beside him, wide-eyed.

"Look at that." Jones drew out each word, awed by the noise and power of the bombardment. He pointed across the river, where white puffs of smoke marked where the shells were striking.

"There they go! Lookit!" Jefferson yelled, so excited that his helmet liner slipped off his head and bounced unnoticed on the ground.

Tanks were rumbling across a shallow place in the river. Or maybe the engineers had put a pontoon bridge across. They were too far away for Jones to tell which. All he could see was the humped dark brown shapes of the Shermans crossing the river.

"Come on, come on! Move it, move it! Let's get rolling!" someone shouted at them.

Without an instant's delay Jones clambered up into the cab of his truck, Jefferson right behind him. As he revved up the engine he looked out the window to see who was making the noise. Wasn't their regular captain, not that high-pitched, squeaky little girl's voice.

There was a jeep beside his truck, with an officer standing straight as a ramrod in the right-hand seat, one hand gripping the top of the windshield to steady himself. An officer with a shining steel helmet emblazoned with three stars, a pair of binoculars around his neck, and a pair of ivory-handled pistols on his hips.

"Jesus Christ, General!" blurted Jones. "Where you think you're goin'? Sir."

"Berlin! I'm going to personally shoot that paperhanging sonofabitch!" Patton was beaming the biggest grin Jones had ever seen on a white man.

The jeep took off with a roar and a cloud of dust, Patton still standing in it. Jones put the truck in gear and lurched off after him.

"That's ol' Blood 'n Guts hisself!" Jefferson yelled, his voice almost as high as Patton's.

"Yeah."

"Who's he gonna shoot? What he say about a paperhangin' sonofabitch?"

"He means Hitler. Hitler worked as a paperhanger before the war, they say."

"No shit?"

"Yeah." The truck bounced along the dirt road, heading down toward the river. Patton still stood straight and tall in front of them.

"Man, I wouldn't want to be no Adolph Hitler when *he* gets to Berlin," Jefferson said fervently.

Chequers, 20 April Churchill took his watch from its pocket in his vest and clicked open its delicate gold cover. Montgomery had been ranting for almost half an hour.

The bantam-sized field marshal had flown from his command post in Germany to the Prime Minister's country residence to make one last plea for Berlin. He looked the very picture of a dashing general, from his rakish beret to his chest full of ribbons down to his perfectly laced combat boots. He had charged headlong into a battle of words the instant he had been ushered into the book-lined study of the country home. He was going to capture Berlin, but before he could do that he needed to capture the support of his Prime Minister.

Churchill knew it was hopeless, but out of his respect for Sir Bernard's past service he allowed the victor of El Alamein to blow off as much steam as he wanted to. After all, Churchill mused to himself, when you are going to kill a man it costs you nothing to be polite about it. I created this situation when I decided to go ahead with Broadsword. Of course the Americans would want the honor of taking Berlin. I should have foreseen that they would. Unfortunately, the decision came as a complete shock to Monty.

"It isn't fair, Winston!" Montgomery was shouting. "It's a stab in the back. Berlin should be *mine!* You know that. I know that. Even Ike knows it. But Bradley and Patton have always schemed against me."

Churchill puffed quietly on his cigar and looked out the window to the soft green countryside. He wished he could be out there with his oil paints; even laying bricks to build another garden wall would be so soothing. Instead, he sat in a wing chair stiff with age and smelling of horsehair and listened to his finest general screeching like a stuck pig.

Montgomery had not been privy to Broadsword; the fewer people who knew that Stalin was assassinated, the better. But Monty was no fool. As soon as the news of Stalin's death became known he was on Eisenhower's back, demanding Berlin as a prize that he had earned by right.

Perhaps so, Churchill thought wearily. But the relationship has changed. The Americans are in the driver's seat now, young and strong and just beginning to realize how powerful they really are. Franklin already treats me with a noticeable condescension. Noblesse oblige. He doesn't even realize he's doing it. What would Franklin say if I told him that I caused Stalin's death; that I have handed the United States mastery of the whole world. To save Britain. To save all that we have striven for over so many centuries. To keep alight the flame of democracy.

There was no other way, Churchill told himself. None whatsoever. Fighting Hitler has exhausted Britain. And I did not bring the British people through this hell merely to hand half the world to Stalin and his odious ilk. Better to give it all to the Americans. Much better for everyone, even the Russians.

The Prime Minister almost smiled. But Monty doesn't think so. He can't see any further than his own desire to be crowned the hero of the war. We've snatched his laurel wreath away from him, and he is justly furious.

Churchill opened his pocket watch again. Just over thirty minutes since Monty had begun his tirade.

"I won't have it!" Montgomery was yelling, his voice thin and nerve-rattling. "I simply won't have it!"

"That's enough," Churchill said.

He said it softly, almost sadly. But the words stopped Montgomery in full flight, with both fists clenched over his head.

"Sit down, Monty," said Churchill.

The field marshal sat.

"There's nothing for it. Patton will take Berlin. Eisenhower has made it clear that if I try to insist that you take the city, he will send his resignation to Washington."

"He'd resign?" Montgomery's face was a mixture of surprise and anxiety.

Churchill nodded heavily. "I'm afraid that if it comes to a choice between you and Ike, the Americans will naturally favor their own man."

"Yes, of course."

"I cannot allow that to happen. I will not force the issue. Patton will take Berlin. You—and I—will have to swallow that hard fact."

Monty's face turned red. "I'll go to the press, dammit. I'll tell them how the bloody Yanks are bullying us!"

"You will do nothing of the sort," Churchill said firmly. "No one will threaten this alliance. Neither you nor I nor anyone else. We are tied to the Americans with bonds of blood. No one of us will try to weaken those bonds. Not while I live and serve His Majesty."

The blood drained from Montgomery's face. "But Berlin. For God's sake, Winston. . . ."

Churchill realized his cigar had gone out. He looked down at its stub, chewed and wet on one end, burned out on the other. There's symbolism for you, he thought.

Looking up into Montgomery's drawn, sad eyes, he said, "I have no idea of what God wants, but I know that the political necessities of the day make it imperative that we acquiesce to Eisenhower's decision. No amount of argument is going to change that. Do I make myself clear, Monty?"

"Yes, sir. Quite clear." It looked as if the field marshal might burst into tears.

Churchill watched him get up from his chair and walk across the ancient carpeting to the door. Let the Yanks have Berlin, Churchill said to himself. It doesn't matter which of us takes the city, as long as it's not the Reds. Let the Yanks do it. Let them take the casualties. We will accomplish our political goal without sacrificing a single British life.

Yet he felt defeated. No, Churchill thought, I feel more like a soldier who has been carrying the colors through the thick of the battle and now that the battle is almost won I've been shot down, mortally wounded, and must pass the flag to another.

Mortally wounded? You're becoming melodramatic in your old age, Winston, Churchill growled to himself. No, worse. You're becoming self-pitying. Brace up! You've won your goal, even if no one will ever know it except yourself.

23

Erfurt, 20 April   "Berlin! You must be crazy!"

Sergeant Kinder shook his head woefully. "That's the scoop. We're going to drop on Berlin. Give Hitler a little birthday present."

Hollis had known it was going to be bad when the truck convoy from France had left them at an airfield. They had a real barracks—a bit shot up by the flyboys before the Army took it away from the Germans—but it had a roof that hardly leaked at all and pretty solid walls and even a stove that kept the night chill out, if you were close enough to it.

"But Berlin?" he asked Kinder. "Why don't they just drop us into an erupting volcano and get it over with?"

Kinder put his fists on his hips and stared the men into sullen silence. They were grouped around him by the black iron stove in the middle of the wooden barracks. Hollis, Jarvick, Loller, Sanderson—he knew these guys. They griped the way all soldiers do, but they were steady and reliable. Even Kaplan, with the nastiest tongue in the platoon; Kinder knew he could count on Kap when the bullets were flying. It was the new men he was worried about. Kids. Teenagers. They looked damned scared.

"Now listen up," he said, once the grumbling had stopped. "Patton's making a breakthrough and racing for Berlin. The Russians are on the east side of the city, ten, twenty miles away at most. Our job is to block the main highways comin' out of the city to the west, so's the Krauts can't move troops from the east to go against Patton."

"Holy Jesus Christ on a crutch," somebody muttered.

Kinder gave them his best lopsided grin. "Come on, now. You dogfaces are official heroes, aintcha? 'The Screamin' Eagles.' 'The Battered Bastards of Bastogne.' Now you're gonna be the first guys into Berlin. It's a fuckin' honor."

Hollis shot back, "Why don't you tell McAuliffe to let somebody else have the fuckin' honor this time?"

"You know what they say," Kinder replied, unruffled. "The shortest road home . . ."

"Is through Berlin, yeah I know."

The men dispersed slowly to their bunks, muttering, grumbling. Hollis saw Jarvick sitting on the edge of his bunk, bent almost double over a flimsy sheet of V-mail paper he was writing on.

"Last will and testament?" Hollis wisecracked.

Jarvick looked up, his face showing surprise and something close to anger. But he calmed down immediately. "No," he said. "Just writing home."

"To the wife?"

"Yes. Don't you have somebody to write to?" It was commonplace that the troops wrote more letters on the eve of a major action than any other time.

"Me? Sure, I got hundreds of women I could write to,"

Hollis replied, standing over Jarvick, grinning crookedly. "That's my problem. I don't which of 'em I should start with."

"Maybe you ought to publish a newspaper for them," Jarvick said.

Hollis laughed. "Now that's not a bad idea. Not bad at all."

Jarvick watched him walk away from the bunk and head for the inevitable card game that was forming up. Not a care in the world, he thought. But he knew better. Hollis is just as scared as I am. He just disguises it better.

For several moments Jarvick watched Hollis make his way through the barracks, attracting fellow gamblers as he went. Then Jarvick stared down at the fountain pen in his hand. He had kept it supplied with ink, one way or another, all the way from Iowa. He knew what he wanted to write: the kind of letter that Cyrano de Bergerac wrote to Roxane. "Goodbye, my love, for today I die."

The censors would never let that through. Even if he put it in as a quote from literature, they wouldn't know who Cyrano was. Jarvick took a deep breath and began to write:

"Dearest Judine: I'm fine. We've been based in a barracks for a change, with a real roof over our heads. It's quite comfortable. . . ."

He wanted to tell her that the war would probably be over by the time she got this letter, but he figured the censors would black that out too. He wanted to tell her that he would be home very soon, but he feared terribly that he would arrive home in a coffin.

Lubben, 20 April Some fifty miles southeast of Berlin, just outside the town of Lubben on the River Spree, Sergeant Alexei Alexandrovich Petrovitch lay on his belly in a roadside ditch, pressing his face into the dirt, clawing with his bare hands toward the center of the Earth. The German artillery barrage was a complete surprise; the Germans weren't even supposed to have any heavy artillery remaining. But the shells were suddenly falling all around him, blasting the ground into a chaos of smoking craters. They're not supposed to have any guns left, Petrovitch snarled to himself as he hugged the moist warm earth. They told us there was nothing facing us except old men and boys armed with obsolete rifles.

The long angry sigh of incoming shells. Petrovitch clawed deeper at the ground, fingertips already bleeding. He had no idea of how many men in his squad might have been hit. He had no idea how long they had been pinned here by the German artillery. It seemed like years had gone by with no relief.

The explosions shook the ground and he heard the evil whine of shrapnel whizzing through the air. This isn't supposed to be happening! he screamed silently to himself. We're supposed to be advancing, not pinned down by artillery the enemy isn't supposed to have. The captain will be furious that we haven't been able to move forward. The political commissar might start shooting sergeants again.

The earth-shaking roar dwindled somewhat, like a thunderstorm moving slowly away. Cautiously Petrovitch raised his head and peered over the ridge of the ditch into the black night. He heard the softer sigh of outgoing rounds fired by the Red Army artillery units far to the rear. Counter-battery fire; about time. The distant horizon lit up with explosions, orange and white and a sullen glowering red. Good! Let the Nazis get a taste of their own medicine.

But once the distant rumbling thunder died away, Petrovitch heard a sound that froze his blood. The roar of diesel engines, the clanking jingling of caterpillar treads.

Tanks! Coming toward him. The Germans weren't supposed to have any more tanks, either.

"Tanks!" he whispered hoarsely to his right and then his left. In the darkness he sensed his men hunkering down deeper into the ditch.

"Their last half-dozen panzers," one of the men muttered acidly. "Again."

"Heavy weapons platoon to the front," he heard an officer calling.

No one responded. The heavy weapons men, with their antitank rockets, must have been hit hardest by the artillery barrage. Most of the rounds had fallen behind Petrovitch's unit, where the rocket men had been moving up.

"We'll have to stop them ourselves," Petrovitch said to the men on either side of him. "Pass the word."

Stop tanks with machine guns and hand grenades? Not likely. But that was all they had. They had used the last rounds for their Siminov the day before, on what their political officer had assured them was absolutely "the last half-dozen of the Panzers."

The seconds ticked by and the sound of the approaching tanks grew louder. Petrovitch kept hoping they would hit another section of the line, but something in his guts told him they were coming straight for this spot, exactly where he lay trembling and wide-eyed, staring into the darkness for his first glimpse of approaching death.

And there they were, huge monstrous clanking growling fortresses of moving steel, prowling through the night, long gun barrels poking out like the probing feelers of giant beetles. Tiger tanks, moving like dinosaurs of steel, lords of the battlefield.

Petrovitch's machine gunners started shooting at the tanks, to no effect. He saw sparks flare where the bullets bounced off the heavy armor. The machine guns in the tanks began to reply, red sputtering gouts of flame sending bullets splattering into the soft earth along the ridge of the ditch. Petrovitch heard men cursing and screaming over the yammering chatter of the machine guns. One of his men leaped up and ran at the tanks, grenades in each hand, instantly cut down by the showers of lead flying through the air. The grenades went off in dull thumps and a brief flash of white, harmless to the tanks, fatal to the soldier bearing them.

One of the Tigers came to the ditch not twenty meters from where Petrovitch lay. He pulled a grenade from his belt, yanked the pin and hurled it at the exposed bogey wheels and tread. He pushed his face into the dirt as the grenade went off, felt white-hot shards of shrapnel rake his back.

There was no pain. No time for it. The tank had ground to a halt, although others were rumbling past the ditch, across the road, and deeper into the night. Petrovitch jumped up, roaring with exultation, and raced to the crippled tank. The grenade had blown off its tread; it could not move, although its crew was still alive inside and its forward machine gun was blazing. The turret was turning slowly in his direction.

Petrovitch ducked under the long cannon barrel and clambered up onto the front of the Tiger. Poking the muzzle of his submachine gun into the first eye slit he saw, he fired off a few rounds. Screams from inside. In training, he had been shown an empty tank painted white inside; his instructor had fired a single pistol shot through one of the open ports. The bullet ricocheted off the steel walls inside until almost all the white paint had been scraped off.

Petrovitch climbed up to the turret and fired a few more

rounds into the eye slit there. No more screams. The first burst had done the job. Then he realized how lucky he was that his bullets had not set off the ammunition inside the tank.

"Comrade sergeant! Your back! It's a mess!"

Shakily, Petrovitch slid back down to the ground. One of his men, so new to the squad that the sergeant had not yet learned his name, was staring wide-eyed at him.

"Never mind my back," he shouted gruffly. "There'll be infantry coming up behind the Tigers. Get the men back into a defensive line along the ditch. Quickly!"

The soldier scuttled off into the night. Petrovitch surveyed the situation. The tanks would continue their penetration; they were going after the artillery and other rear elements. He smiled grimly. The officers and staff men at headquarters were going to have to do some fighting, for a change.

Then he took a deep, painful breath. So will we. The infantry will be following the tanks.

He took a step away from the tank, but his legs no longer had the strength to hold him up. He collapsed face first onto the ground, unconscious and bleeding heavily.

Kustrin, 20 April   "Counterattack?" Field Marshal Zhukov spat out the word. "Where?"

"Just east of Lubben," said his aide, a flimsy yellow sheet of paper from the radio operator in his fist. Zhukov noted that despite the grim expression on the redheaded captain's face his hands were not shaking.

"Lubben? Exactly at the seam between our front and Koniev's!"

"They always have had excellent intelligence."

The other officers and men in the low-roofed dugout were

silent, watching their commander. There was no battle to be heard outside, nothing but the eternal chirping of crickets in the shattered remains of what had been a forest.

Zhukov strode to the map table and bent over it. "What strength? What direction?"

The captain peered at the yellow sheet for a moment, then answered, "There are no details."

Zhukov snatched it from his hands. The typing said: "Heavy counterattack before Lubben. Artillery and tanks. Request permission to withdraw to river."

Hitler truly is mad, Zhukov thought. To send what few remaining tanks he has into a counterattack. We'll stop them at the Neisse and chew them up just the way the Americans did in the Bulge.

Then he remembered, It was the Americans and the British at the Bulge. Montgomery and Bradley worked together then. I'll need Koniev's help to destroy the salient. With him hitting them from the south and me from the north, we can wipe out the last of Hitler's panzer forces.

But I can't order Koniev to attack the southern flank of the salient. The orders will have to come from Moscow. From Khrushchev, if he's still in charge of the Red Army today. They keep changing everything in Moscow. It's all a turmoil back there.

Cottbus, 20 April   Field Marshal Koniev was also bending over a map in his forward headquarters, on the back of an American truck, with sides and roof of armor plate: slow, but mobile.

"So they're counterattacking at Lubben," he said. "Good. Excellent."

His staff clustered around him in the poorly ventilated truck. Cigarette smoke hung heavily in the air. From outside came a distant booming that sounded almost like thunder, but too regular and too prolonged to be anything natural.

"Zhukov will need our help on the southern flank of the salient," said one of the officers, a heavyset graying man with the thick features of a peasant.

"Or we could move here," said the colonel on Koniev's left, tracing a line across the map with the stub of an amputated finger, "along this axis, and pinch off the Nazis."

Koniev shook his head. "Have any orders come in from Moscow?"

"Not yet. It is too soon. The counterattack began only five hours ago."

"And already Zhukov is pulling back to the Neisse?"

"Yes. He's drawing the Nazis in, apparently. Then he'll cut them off and annihilate them. With our help, of course."

Koniev straightened up. He was much taller than the others, and younger than anyone with the rank of colonel or higher.

"Comrades, our goal is not to help Zhukov but to take Berlin. This Nazi counterattack is a blessing for us. We will move across the River Spree *now*, while the Hitlerites are busy annoying Zhukov. Then we drive north, along the Luckenwalde-Potsdam-Berlin line. We can be in Berlin within a few days!"

"But the counterattack? Zhukov needs our help."

"By circling around the counterattacking Nazis we cut off their supply routes. That will take the pressure off Zhukov. Let him deal with the salient while we drive to Berlin."

The oldest man in the cramped compartment, a general who had been at Leningrad and now served as Koniev's chief of communications, gave the field marshal a somber frown.

"We must get approval from Moscow for this," he said.

"By all means!" Koniev said grandly. "Send them our

plan at once." Turning to his chief of operations, a much younger man, he added, "Start the forward elements at dawn. I want to be across the Spree and moving north by northwest before Moscow wakes up."

"Suppose Moscow orders us to help Zhukov against this counterattack?" the old general asked.

"I will tell Moscow that we are doing precisely that—by driving on Berlin," said Koniev.

24

Berlin, 20 April "It goes well," said Hitler, bending over the tabletop map.

General Heinrici nodded. "Surprisingly well. They did not expect a Panzer attack."

"And Koniev is giving no indication of moving to help Zhukov, is he?"

"None whatsoever, my Führer."

Hitler clapped his hands together and rubbed them happily. "You see, Heinrici? I give myself the best birthday present of them all. We have them on the run."

Heinrici smiled. It certainly seemed so. Zhukov's front lines had been penetrated and the Russians seemed to be falling back in disarray. Not a route, but not a planned, orderly retreat, either. It all depended on what Koniev would do.

And then there were the Americans.

"My Führer, I should remind you that the Americans have crossed the Elbe and are driving toward Berlin."

"A feint," Hitler said, contemptuously. "Eisenhower is trying to frighten us into moving troops away from the eastern front. Nothing more than a feint."

Heinrici was going to say that intelligence reports indicated this "feint" might be General Patton's entire Third Army. But at that moment the doors at the far end of the situation room banged open and Goebbels came in, little gnomish man with a slight limp.

"Happy birthday, my Führer!" Goebbels proclaimed.

Eva Braun and Frau Goebbels were right behind him, with Martin Bormann and a crowd of officers, clerks, and SS guards. Eva was carrying a small cake glowing with candles. Others bore trays of food and buckets of champagne.

Heinrici gave up all attempts to continue the military discussion. Hitler was fifty-six years old this day, though he appeared twenty years older. He could not blow out all the candles, he had not the breath even for the five that were perched on the cake. His hands shook as he accepted a cup of coffee. He could not remain standing for more than a few minutes.

Let him rest, Heinrici thought as an SS guard held a stool for the Führer to sit upon. He's carried all these burdens for so long. Let him rest for a little while, at least. If he's going to pull off a miracle and save us all, it won't hurt to let him have a few moments of happiness and rest.

Heinrici accepted a fluted glass of champagne: French champagne, he noted. And there was caviar from the Caspian. He looked at the silver trays of food, the finest from every part of Europe. All the nations we had conquered, he thought. We had all of Europe in our grasp, but now it has been wrested away from us. And Germany herself is being ground into dust by the advancing Allies.

The general shook his head wearily. This isn't war anymore, it's destruction, pure and simple. We should surrender and get it over with. Even the miracle of Stalin's death won't help us, not with Patton breaking through and heading for Berlin.

For a moment he thought that if only the Führer were somehow removed, taken out of the picture, then Germany might be able to make an honorable peace with the Allies. But not with him in power, Heinrici knew. And he knew he would do nothing to remove his Führer. He had only contempt for the cowards who had stooped to assassination and botched even that. We have all sworn an oath of loyalty to the Führer himself, a personal oath that no man worthy of a general's rank could even think of breaking. No matter what. We were with him when he was winning, and now we must remain with him. To the death.

Goebbels, meanwhile, was giving a speech extolling their Führer's many virtues, dwelling on the victories that had swept all of Europe and promising better days to come.

"Even now," said the propaganda minister, "the Bolsheviks are reeling back in confusion and retreat, thanks to our Führer's masterful military genius."

Everyone dutifully toasted Hitler's military genius. Even Heinrici, who knew that the counterattack on which Goebbels placed such high hopes would soon run out of steam.

Then Hitler started a rambling, reminiscent talk about the old days when the Party was so small that their entire headquarters could fit in a clothes closet. Eva laughed and beamed at him and ate three pieces of cake. Everyone seemed happy. Except Bormann. To Heinrici, the Führer's secretary looked like a wild boar: big undershot jaw, darting feral eyes. A dangerous man, always scheming, always trying to protect his master from bad news.

Hitler's speech grew more somber. A rumble of bombs and shells shook the bunker. He glanced up at the concrete ceiling, both hands balled into fists.

"From the beginning," he said, "I have known that this would be a life-or-death struggle for the German people. I knew it at the time of the Putsch in 'Twenty-three. I knew that if the German people would follow me fearlessly with all their strength, we would conquer the enemies that surrounded us. I would lead them to true greatness, to a Reich that would last a thousand years, bigger and more glorious than any empire the world has ever seen!"

No one said a word. There was no sound in the bunker except the muted roar of the bombardment going on overhead.

"But the German people have failed me," Hitler said, with a bitter shake of his head. "They lack the strength to be true rulers. They lack the will to persevere and conquer no matter what the obstacles. Very well! They have failed. Let them perish. If they cannot be the rulers then they deserve to be extinguished from the pages of history. Let them perish, I say! Let the entire nation be destroyed, all of it, down to the smallest village and farmstead. I could have led them to greatness but they have failed. Now they deserve to be wiped out, erased totally. I want every building destroyed, every factory leveled, every bridge blown up. The Bolsheviks and the traitorous British and those mongrel Americans must find nothing! Nothing! I bequeath them a Germany that is dead and burning. That is what the German people deserve and that is what I will give them. Not a stick is to remain standing, do you hear?"

He was not screaming, as he so often did when he worked himself into one of his tirades. This speech was cold and calm, absolutely chilling to all who stood there, the champagne going flat in their glasses, their faces white, their mouths hanging open.

Eva Braun could not hide her sobs and she ran from the room. Hitler sagged onto the stool that Bormann held for him, shaking his head and muttering to himself. All the others, even Goebbels, began to file out of the room in stunned silence.

But as they headed toward their private quarters and personal fears in the dank underground bunker, Hitler clutched at Bormann's arm.

Pulling him away from the others, Hitler said softly, "I have a special duty for you to perform, Bormann."

"Yes, my Führer?"

Lowering his voice even further, Hitler said, "It must be kept totally secret. No one else must know. Only you and me."

Bormann nodded as if he knew what was coming.

Whispering now, Hitler said, "If worst comes to worst, if the Russians break in here and threaten to capture this fortress . . ." he hesitated, glancing around to see that no one was within earshot. "I want you to shoot me."

"But we are driving the swine backward."

"Better to be dead than a prisoner of the Bolsheviks," Hitler continued, as if he had not heard Bormann. "You are to shoot me, and Miss Braun, as well. We have discussed this. She says she will take poison, if it comes to that, but she is a woman and weak. You must make certain that neither of us falls into the hands of the Russians. We must not be taken prisoner."

"I understand," Bormann said.

"Goebbels will take care of himself and his family. I know him. He has already acquired the cyanide capsules for his wife and each of his children."

"Surely, my Führer, things will not get that bad. Your counterattack—"

"Perhaps it will succeed. Perhaps not. In war we must be prepared to make sacrifices. Do you understand me?"

"Yes, my Führer."

"And burn my body afterward. Scatter my ashes to the winds. If the German people are not strong enough to conquer their enemies, then I will die among them and leave nothing for our enemies to gloat over."

Genthin, 22 April   Staff Sergeant Al Rosenberg sat on the lip of his Sherman's turret hatch as they rumbled through the town. He should have been happy, but as he looked out at the rows of three- and four-story houses they were passing a growing anger simmered inside him.

House after house showed the white flag of surrender. White towels, white tablecloths, even whole bedsheets were dangling from the upper story windows as the long row of dust-covered tanks clanked through the town.

It's been this way since we broke across the Elbe, Rosenberg grumbled to himself. Fucking Krauts giving up without a fight. All we have to do is show up and they quit.

Rosenberg had been among the troops that had liberated Buchenwald. He had not been able to sleep without seeing those emaciated, horror-ridden prisoners of the Third Reich. Their crime had been that they were Jews. Their punishment had been the cruelest hell that any human being had ever devised.

And these fine Aryans, these people whom Hitler had declared to be a warrior race, fit to conquer and enslave the whole world, now they were quitting without a fight.

Rosenberg's guts churned with rage. Come on and fight, you bastards. Take a shot at me. See, I'm perched up here out in the open. You must have a couple of soldiers hiding in some basement. Maybe a sniper up in the church tower there. Come on, shoot at me! Just one shot. Give me a reason to pop back inside and start pumping cannon shells into your goddamned smug-ass houses. Let me kill a few of you, you murdering sonsofbitches. Just a few. Like maybe a million or two.

Then he thought, Berlin's less than fifty miles up the road. They'll fight when we get to Berlin. That's where the Kraut army's waiting for us. Hitler, too. They say he's still in Berlin.

Wait for me, Adolf, he prayed fervently. Wait for me in Berlin, you cocksucking bastard. Just wait for me to get there.

25

Moscow, 22 April   It still felt odd to Molotov to sit at the head of the table. After so many years, his whole lifetime, really, of watching Stalin run things, now he sat at the head of the table.

But he did not rule by himself, of course. The one thing that they had decided on immediately upon Stalin's unexpected death was that there would no longer be a one-man rule. The committee would run things, in true Soviet fashion. That was why Beria had to go. He would have stepped into Stalin's shoes at once. He would have started his own reign of terror until he felt satisfied that no one was left alive who might oppose him. Nikita cut him down before he could act against us. It was kill or be killed, pure and simple.

Now, as the legitimate prime minister of the Soviet government, Molotov sat at the head of the table. Closely flanked by Khrushchev and Malenkov.

"The commanders in the field cannot simply go running

off on their own," Khrushchev was saying. "That way will lead to chaos and defeat."

"Defeat?" Malenkov almost sneered. Always chubby, he seemed to have gained weight in the few days since the Great One's untimely death. "The Hitlerites don't have enough left to defeat anyone. It's merely a matter of time."

"And lives," Khrushchev added pointedly.

Malenkov shrugged.

Molotov knew he held the balance of power between the two men. Malenkov was in favor of allowing Koniev to race for Berlin. Khrushchev wanted to order Koniev to help eliminate the Lubben salient that the Nazis had driven into Zhukov's lines.

"Comrades," he said, "may I remind you that at this very moment General Patton is scarcely seventy kilometers from Berlin? Do we want to see the Americans snatch the prize away from us?"

Khrushchev started to reply, then thought better of it. He sank back into his chair, grumbling something under his breath. Malenkov smiled at the prime minister. My god, Molotov thought, he almost looks like a woman when he smiles that way.

"Then it is decided?" Molotov asked. "Koniev continues on to Berlin while Zhukov deals with the Nazi salient on his own."

"Yes," Malenkov said immediately.

Khrushchev scratched at his bald pate, then reluctantly answered, "Yes."

Molotov let a small sigh of satisfaction escape his lips. Now to get to Berlin before the Americans do.

Malenkov felt satisfied. Koniev was an old friend, and an important ally in the struggles to come within the Kremlin.

Khrushchev kept the disappointed frown on his face, but he thought to himself that Zhukov represented the Red

Army much more so than Koniev. The top officers adored Zhukov and distrusted Koniev. Let Koniev go to Berlin; Hitler's desperate forces trapped inside the city will make the battle a bloody shambles. When Koniev's troops bog down inside the city Zhukov can come to his rescue and snatch the glory from him. Meanwhile Zhukov will keep the respect of the officer corps, and I will keep Zhukov bound closely to me. When push comes to shove, when I make my move against Malenkov, I will have the best part of the army behind me.

Khrushchev had to exert an effort of will to keep from smiling. Malenkov will have Koniev, but how surprised he will be to find that Koniev will have no one to back him up.

A few blocks northeast of the Kremlin, past the huge and echoingly empty GUM department store, Ivan Petrovitch Gretchko sat at his desk in the Ministry for State Security, frowning unhappily.

Gretchko was a colonel in the MGB. And a deeply puzzled and worried man.

He sat in his office, slowly smoking a thin cigarette and staring out the window. He paid no attention to the few people walking on Lubyanka Square outside or those sitting on the benches, enjoying the warmth of the wan April sun. He did not even pay the slightest attention to the pair of women who had opened their winter coats, showing nothing but abbreviated bathing suits beneath so they could catch as much precious sunshine as possible.

Gretchko's eyes saw nothing of this because his mind was concentrating furiously on the problem. *The* problem. There was nothing else on earth that occupied his attention these past ten days. Not even the turmoil within the Ministry since Beria's death. MGB officers were being reassigned, transferred, even sent to the front lines. Several of his friends had disappeared altogether; the rumor was that they had been sent to Siberia, either by Malenkov or Khrushchev. Or perhaps one of the other high-and-mighty ones in the Kremlin. Everything was upside down. No one knew who was really in charge.

None of that bothered Gretchko, even though he knew he should be worried about his friends, his associates, his own position within the Ministry. But he resolutely kept those fears out of his mind, concentrating instead on *the* problem, the problem of Josef Stalin's death.

Could it have been murder? Assassination? If so, by whom?

Gretchko was not a detective in the usual sense. His normal job was analysis of intelligence reports. While popular novels and films dealt with spies and their romantic adventures, Gretchko knew that the business of intelligence depended on analysis more than spying. Any dolt or drunkard or homosexual could be turned into a spy by bribery or bullying. Or flattery. Or even for supposedly higher motives. It always astounded Gretchko how easy it was to get a man or a woman to turn traitor. He had nothing but contempt for such people.

No, spying meant nothing without analysis. There were thousands of agents out there, millions of them, perhaps. All digging and worming and weaseling scraps of information and then sending it on to Moscow. Most of what they sent was nonsense or actual misinformation planted by the enemy. Even the good material was useless by itself. It took careful analysis to piece together all the little scraps until they made a coherent picture. Gretchko pictured himself as a master craftsman, an artist, even: taking the minuscule gleanings from all around the world and creating a clear and accurate picture from them.

His favorite form of art was mosaics. His favorite relaxation was jigsaw puzzles.

It was the report from England that worried him. By itself it meant little. But put it together with other factors and a picture began to emerge.

The Americans sent a small sample of something called plutonium to England nearly two years ago, just before the Tehran Conference. Gretchko had only the vaguest idea of what plutonium was, or what the Americans were doing with it. He knew of the Manhattan Project and the effort to make a bomb powerful enough to level an entire city. How the bomb worked or what made it so powerful was not a matter for his department.

He had learned, however, that this plutonium stuff was deadly. Like radium, it gave off invisible rays that could kill a man. A microscopic amount of it could be fatal. You did not have to swallow it, either. Just stand in its presence long enough and the rays would kill you. How long? No one seemed to know. Gretchko had spoken to medical doctors and university scientists. None of them knew anything specific enough to be of help.

The worst part of his problem was that he had to work on it by himself. No one else seemed to care. Only Comrade Khrushchev, who would soon be elected Secretary of the Communist Party. He was the only one in the Kremlin, in the entire government as far as Gretchko could tell, who wanted an investigation into the Great One's death.

"You must act alone, comrade Gretchko," Khrushchev had told him, the morning when Stalin's death had been announced.

"Surely you don't suspect that someone would murder the Maximum Leader!" Gretchko had blurted.

Khrushchev surveyed him with narrowed eyes that seemed to penetrate to Gretchko's soul. "You are a good and honest man, comrade colonel. That is apparent from your record, and I can see it for myself."

"Thank you, sir."

"When a great man dies as suddenly as comrade Stalin has," Khrushchev said slowly, "it is wise to examine the cause. In all probability you are correct, and his death was natural. But we must leave no stone unturned, comrade. If it was *not* a natural death, then we have a traitor in our midst. A traitor at the highest level of the Soviet state."

"I see, comrade."

"Leave no stone unturned, colonel. Not even a pebble."

But he's made me work alone, Gretchko thought, taking a long drag on his cigarette. He's relieved me of all other duties and given me *carte blanche* to go wherever I must and interview anyone I wish. Yet I have no aides, no assistants. And I must report directly to Khrushchev in person. Not even written reports will do. I must speak to him face-to-face.

Who does he suspect? He will not say. But obviously he suspects one of his comrades in the Kremlin.

Gretchko did not trust Khrushchev, the man who had Beria shot, one of the men who are purging the MGB. He is attempting to take over the ministry, that seemed certain. So are the others; control the MGB and you control the country. Who will win this struggle? Will they tear the MGB apart while they battle over it? Beria had been a powerful leader; ruthless, yes, but a man who protected his own people. The ministry had grown enormously under his leadership. And Khrushchev cut him down as soon as Stalin died. Was Beria the one Khrushchev suspects? Am I supposed to find out that my former boss was the traitor? Is this a test of my abilities? Of my loyalties?

Gretchko sat pondering the different possibilities until long after the sun had set. I am playing with dynamite here, he knew. If I find that Beria was a traitor it will make an even worse shambles of the MGB. It will be like the purge trials all over again, except that this time *we* will be in the dock. Or what if I find that Molotov or one of the other ministers was the murderer? A man could get himself killed that way.

He spun all the factors around in his mind and always came to the same inescapable conclusion. He had to push ahead with his investigation and let the chips fall where they may. You're the best analyst in the MGB, he told himself. That's why comrade Khrushchev picked you for this job. Now you must show him that he picked the right man. And if narrow-eyed Nikita truly is moving to capture all the Kremlin for himself, then you can rise to the top with him. Perhaps.

The hell of it was that he could not get a fresh autopsy of Stalin's body. The doctors had performed one immediately after his death, and then quickly embalmed the Great One's remains in preparation for placing him beside Lenin in the tomb built into the Kremlin's wall. Not even Khrushchev would authorize another autopsy.

"You'll have to do your best without one," he had told Gretchko. "The medical report was quite detailed. We can't open up the body again, not unless you have a specific idea of what you're looking for. This is Josef Stalin we're speaking of, not some cadaver in a medical school."

At last Gretchko got up from his desk and stretched, arms raised to the ceiling, spine popping like a string of firecrackers.

The report from England. He walked to the window and looked down on the square, deserted now in the early evening darkness.

Why would the Americans send plutonium to the British? Just before the Tehran Conference. Suppose they wanted to assassinate Stalin. The British especially are antirevolutionary reactionaries. Churchill himself represents all the evils of the old imperialist system. Roosevelt is more progressive, yet he himself comes from the privileged class.

Standing by the window, Gretchko let his chain of reasoning play out. Was there something at the Tehran Conference that was significant? Then he remembered the newsreel pictures of Churchill handing Stalin a sword—the Sword of Stalingrad.

Could that have been an assassination weapon? Is it possible that the sample of plutonium the Americans sent to London was put inside the Sword?

Gretchko shook his head. The Sword had been in Stalin's possession for nearly two years. Would the plutonium take that long to kill him? The little he had learned about how radium kills told him that no one would last two years under the lash of those deadly rays.

But did Stalin have the Sword near him all that time? Was it near him when he died? Those were questions that had to be answered.

Taking a deep breath, Gretchko at last felt that he had something to report to Khrushchev. And specific steps to take in his investigation.

26

Potsdam, 23 April   As he hung swaying in his parachute harness, wind rushing past, Jarvick strained his eyes to see the ground rushing up in the first gray light of early dawn. He always felt as if he were dropping like a stone, weighted down by a heavy field pack, damned near a case of ammunition, grenades, the extra chute strapped to his chest, and every piece of field equipment the Army could load onto him, including a brand-new Mark VI lightweight foldable entrenching tool—a goddamned shovel.

They were coming down in a field. Good enough. Back in Normandy half the outfit had landed in flooded swamps. Lots of guys drowned before they could struggle out of their harnesses, pulled down by the eighty-some pounds of crap they each had to carry.

But this was an open field, he could see that much. Some buildings off to the right. Seem to be empty. No shooting.

Not even flak against the planes. Maybe they're saving their ammo to get us just as we land.

But he hit the ground with a heavy thud, rolled over, and began collapsing his chute in nearly total silence. More thuds and grunts and whispered swearing as the rest of the platoon landed. It was getting bright enough to see but still they whispered as if it were night.

Kinder gave a single sharp whistle and they gathered around him. One of the new kids had hurt his leg; sprain or fracture, he couldn't walk on it. Kinder detailed one youngster to stay with him, another to go off and find the medics that had parachuted with them.

"Okay," he told the remaining men, "the next wave of planes'll be dropping the heavy stuff. Spread out and form a perimeter around the drop zone."

Jarvick fell in beside Hollis. DiMaggio, one of the replacements, walked on Jarvick's other side, slightly bent under the weight of his pack, hands gripping his rifle as if he intended to engage in hand-to-hand combat. An Italian kid from California, good-looking in a kind of olive-skinned, wavy-haired way; no relation to the ballplayer but the whole squad called him Joltin' Joe anyway.

They got to the woods at the edge of the field, flopped down and wormed off the heavy packs. Jarvick shoved his pack in front of him as a makeshift protection. No sense digging in, they'd be moving through the woods as soon as the second drop came in. The sky was starting to brighten. Still no sign of Germans. For all the bombing that the flyboys had done in Berlin, just a few miles up the road, the trees here looked almost untouched. Jarvick could see new buds on their upreaching branches.

A dull rumbling sound came up from the distance and grew into the thunder of a flight of C-47s flying almost at

pain burned the length of his spine. The past winter, without heat, without medication, without decent food, had turned his body into a purgatory of pain.

He looked into the faces of his child-warriors. They were not children's faces any more. No grins, no hooting or joking or horseplay. God, the Mausers they carry are bigger than they are, some of them. The word was that the Russians had landed parachute troops somewhere near the park in Potsdam. Their job was to clear them out.

Victory or death. Those were the Führer's words. Victory or death. And to back them up, Himmler had issued an order saying anyone caught attempting to surrender would be shot, and his family would be shot also. As if the Russians aren't killing enough of us, Schacht thought morosely. As if the American and British bombers haven't wiped out all the family I had left.

Victory or death. He knew which it would be. Already their truck convoy had been shot up by American *jabos*. Half their force was already dead or dying in burning trucks, children lying along the highway's shoulders burned, bleeding, torn apart by bullets, whimpering for their mothers.

The trucks stopped. Painfully, like a rusty old screen door, Schacht slowly got to his feet and peered over the edge of the truck's side. The tall old birch and elm trees of the park waved in the morning breeze a hundred meters or so up the highway, their new leaves a bright springtime green.

Colonel Hoerner came thumping back from his staff car. He had lost a leg at Kursk, and his false leg fit him so poorly that he preferred to use a crutch.

"Schacht," he commanded in a blustering, angry voice, "get your men out of that damned truck and scout the edge of the woods. I must know how strong the enemy is."

"Yes, sir, colonel," Schacht replied, thinking, They are stronger than we are, that I can tell you now.

The kids were jumping down from the truck and forming a ragged line when Schacht heard the *pow* sound of an antitank gun. He went flat on the ground and his kids did the same. At least I've trained them that far, he said to himself. An explosion.

Hoerner was flat on his face a few centimeters away, his face red with choler. "My staff car! The swine have destroyed my staff car!"

More artillery rounds were coming their way; Schacht heard the soft deadly whine of howitzer shells, saw them bursting in the air above the trucks, shredding everything with white-hot shrapnel.

"Get away from the trucks!" he screamed to his kids, getting stiffly to his feet. Two of the boys helped the colonel up, and they all hobbled toward the shrubbery that lined the side of the road.

Bullets were whizzing by as they tumbled through the flowering shrubs and down the grassy embankment on the other side. Dazed, Schacht looked around. Half his kids had dropped their guns in their pell-mell rush to get away from the shelling. Colonel Hoerner's crutch was nowhere to be seen.

Through the trees, not a hundred meters in front of them, he could see a squad of enemy soldiers setting up mortars, short ugly stovepipes that would lob more death on the children caught up on the highway by the trucks.

"Follow me," he whispered to his kids. Without looking back to see how many obeyed, he began crawling along the ditch toward the mortar squad. At least we can take them out before they kill us. We can do that much..

With hand signals he deployed his "men" along the edge of the embankment. His back and shoulders felt like fire, but he painfully worked his Mauser to his shoulder and sighted on one of the enemy. Their uniforms looked strange, not like the Russian uniforms he had seen in photos. Their helmets were different, too.

"Fire!" he yelled as he squeezed his trigger.

The enemy soldiers dropped to the ground, whether hit or to protect themselves Schacht could not tell. Within seconds they were returning fire, bullets spattering dirt everywhere, death whining millimeters past his ear.

It was useless, Schacht saw. The kids couldn't hit an elephant; most of them were hunkered down, eyes squeezed shut, terrified by their first experience of a firefight. Schacht marveled that he was not doing the same; it was his first firefight, too.

The shooting stopped, momentarily. He could hear his own ragged breathing, somebody sobbing, whether in pain or fear or both he could not tell. No one seemed to be hit. Not yet. Voices drifted toward them from the woods:

"They're over in the fuckin' ditch!"

"Get the mortars on them."

English! They were speaking English, not Russian! But they didn't sound like Englishmen.

"Are you Americans?" Schacht hollered to them. *"Sind Sie Amerikaner?"*

The enemy troops went quiet.

"Amerikaner?" Schacht yelled again.

"Damned right, Kraut. Americans."

Hoerner was muttering something down at the bottom of the ditch, floundering around like a hooked fish without his crutch. Schacht carefully peered over the edge of the embankment. The planes that had attacked them earlier had been American, not Russian. The uniforms, the helmets. The voices were speaking in American.

He put his rifle down and struggled up to his feet, hands raised over his head.

"Schacht, you fool!" the colonel snarled.

"Put your weapons down," Schacht said to his kids, "and do as I do. That is an order."

Slowly the youngsters obeyed, until they were all standing along the edge of the ditch, hands upraised.

Colonel Hoerner grabbed one of the discarded Mausers and, using it as a crutch, struggled to a standing position. "Schacht, the edict! Himmler's edict!"

"I have no family left alive for the pig to kill," Schacht yelled back. Then, to his kids, "Walk slowly toward the Yankees. Keep your hands raised and we will all live through this day."

It is my responsibility, Schacht said to himself. There is no reason for these boys to be killed. Germany will need her sons after the war.

A pair of Americans walked cautiously out of the shelter of the trees, carbines cradled in their arms. "Okay, come on over here," one of them said, beckoning with one hand. Schacht understood his gesture more than his words.

"Christ, they're just kids," said the other American.

27

Moscow, 28 April   The map room in the Kremlin had not changed at all since Stalin's death. It was next to the small conference room that abutted the late Great One's office. One could go from the office through the conference room and into the map room. No one had dared to assume Stalin's personal office for himself. The office remained closed, like a shrine. Or like a haunted chamber.

But the map room was constantly filled with ministers and their staff assistants. Nikita Khrushchev and Viachislav Molotov stood side by side before the giant wall map of Berlin. Every street, every building was precisely drawn. Red pins marked the advance of Koniev's troops; white ones, Zhukov's. The Americans were in blue.

"It's down to street-by-street fighting now," Khrushchev said. "Like Stalingrad."

"Except that we are the invaders and they the defenders," said Molotov.

They made an incongruous pair. Both short, almost the same height. That was where the similarities ended. Molotov was smartly dressed in a dark pinstripe suit, his thinning hair carefully combed forward to mask his receding hairline. His frame was slight, almost delicate. He took off his pince-nez for a moment, rubbed at his eyes, then perched it back upon the bridge of his nose. Khrushchev wore his usual baggy gray suit. His bald dome glistened in the overhead lights. His narrow little eyes squinted at the map.

Neither man had known sleep for nearly thirty-six hours. They were following the progression of the battle for Berlin; they had taken their meals in this map room, watching, pacing, staring as the uniformed clerks picked up telephones from the bank along the table set against the far wall, listened briefly, then went to the map and moved a pin forward. Or sometimes backward.

The Americans had gotten to Berlin first, after Patton's headlong dash from the Elbe. But once inside the city the German resistance had stiffened fiercely. Koniev had pushed into the city's southern suburbs while Zhukov demolished the counterattack at Lubben, then rolled into Berlin from the east.

"It is only a matter of time," said Molotov, with a weary sigh.

"And then what?" Khrushchev asked, his eyes on the pretty female clerk who had to stand on tiptoes to move one of Zhukov's units a single street forward.

"Then it is over, at last."

Khrushchev waggled a stubby finger in Molotov's face. "No, comrade. Then it begins."

Molotov's brows rose questioningly.

"This troika we have created cannot last. Malenkov doesn't have the strength to help us lead the country."

As if he were hearing something he had long expected, Molotov asked, "What do you suggest?"

"I will be elected general secretary of the Party next week. I would like you to consider taking the foreign ministry again."

"And Malenkov?"

"We'll find something useful for him to do." Khrushchev's heavy peasant features took on a canny look. "Make him chief of the interior ministry. Let him spend his time traveling in Siberia and the Moslem republics, inspecting dams and bridges."

Molotov smiled, something he did but rarely.

Khrushchev excused himself from the map room and walked down the busy corridor of the Presidium building, bustling with men and women in uniform, crossed the wind-swept street and stepped into the green-domed Council of Ministers building, where his own office was.

It was somewhat calmer in the Ministers' building. Most of the people in the corridors were in civilian clothes. They all instantly recognized comrade Khrushchev and smiled their greetings to him. He grinned back at them, gap-toothed.

Gretchko was waiting in his outer office, sitting with ill-concealed impatience on the chair beside his private secretary's desk. She had a fistful of telegrams to hand him, but Khrushchev waved her off and motioned for Gretchko to come with him into the private inner office.

"I'm sorry to keep you waiting, comrade colonel," said Khrushchev as he went to the broad, leather-topped desk and plopped into its big creaking chair. "The battle rages night and day, you know."

Gretchko had asked to see him nearly a week ago. Each passing day his requests had become more urgent.

"Now then," Khrushchev said, placing his hands flat on the desk top, "what have you discovered?"

Gretchko took the armchair in front of the desk. "Perhaps 'discovered' is too strong a word, comrade secretary."

Khrushchev grinned. "Ah, after nearly a week of bombarding me with requests for a meeting it turns out that your information is not that urgent after all."

"I wouldn't say that, exactly."

"And I'm not the general secretary yet, you know. Only the acting secretary."

Gretchko's brows pulled together unhappily. He had a long narrow face, almost triangular, Khrushchev noticed. Broad brow and pointed chin. Large intelligent eyes; on a woman they would be beautiful.

Khrushchev took a cigarette from the box on his desk and offered the box to Gretchko. "American. Good tobacco."

The intelligence analyst took one and they both lit up. Waving smoke from his face, Khrushchev said, "So, what is it that you wanted to tell me?"

"I think I know what killed comrade Stalin."

"Not a stroke?"

"Yes, it might have been a stroke, but it was caused by something. It was not natural."

Khrushchev's narrow eyes glittered. "What do you mean, comrade?"

"This is mostly supposition," Gretchko said. "There are very few facts to go on."

"Tell me what you think."

Hunching forward in the chair, Gretchko said, "I believe that you were right, comrade. Stalin did not die a natural death. He was murdered."

"How? By whom?"

"I don't know who, not yet. But I think I know how. He was poisoned—"

"Nonsense! That was the first thing the doctors looked for in the autopsy. He died of a stroke."

"He was poisoned by radiation," Gretchko said.

"What?"

Slowly, patiently, Gretchko explained his theory. He went over what he knew about radiation poisoning and its effects on the body. He reviewed the report from London about the plutonium. He reminded Khrushchev about the Sword of Stalingrad.

"Yes," said Khrushchev, his face darkening, "I have seen the Sword in his office, myself. I think it's still there."

"It may have been the murder weapon," Gretchko said.

"How could you prove this?"

Raising a long finger, Gretchko replied, "First, I would examine the Sword to see if the plutonium sample is in it."

"Surely the assassins would have removed it to prevent its being discovered."

"Probably so, comrade. But there would still be residual radiation in the Sword itself, from the plutonium. Quite a bit of radiation, I should think. It could easily be detected by the devices the scientists have."

"I see."

Another finger, "Second, I would examine comrade Stalin's body once more to look for the effects of radiation poisoning. That would clinch the matter."

"Yes," said Khrushchev. "It would, wouldn't it?"

Gretchko leaned back in the armchair and let out a deep breath.

Khrushchev asked, "So you think that the British—Churchill himself—deliberately assassinated comrade Stalin?"

"The British, with American help. Yes. Even if Churchill

personally knew nothing of it, someone high in the British government did. Frankly, I can't believe that Churchill knew nothing. He must have approved the plot, at least."

"But that still means that there must have been one or more of our own people involved in the plot, doesn't it?"

"Not necessarily," said Gretchko. "But it would be a good idea to check on all of the Great One's staff. Especially his closest aides. See if any of them have been effected by radiation poisoning."

"Yes. That is a good idea."

Gretchko stubbed out the remains of his cigarette in the ash stand next to his chair. "I know that this may all be pure fantasy, comrade. But at least we can check on the Sword to see if I'm right. If it's radioactive, then we will have to proceed further."

Khrushchev nodded, then got to his feet. Leaning across his desk he extended a stubby arm toward Gretchko.

"Good work, comrade colonel," he said, shaking the younger man's hand once Gretchko stood up. "I will attend to this immediately."

Gretchko nodded, looked as if he wanted to say something more, but then shut his mouth and went to the door.

"I'll keep you informed," promised Khrushchev. "You have done an excellent job."

"Thank you, comrade."

Gretchko left, closing the door softly behind him. Khrushchev sank back into his chair again.

The British assassinated Stalin? With American help? He marveled at the immensity of the idea. This could tear apart our alliance. It could make enemies of us—if the others ever find out.

It had been an idea of pure genius to put a man like Gretchko on the problem. If he can puzzle out what happened, then others can, given time.

Time is important now, Khrushchev told himself. I can't allow our alliance with the West to break up until the Hitlerites are totally defeated. Let the Americans break their backs on Japan, we have a decade of reconstruction ahead of us. What the Soviet Union needs now is a time of peace, so we can rebuild and heal the wounds of this damned war. This is no time to go accusing Churchill of assassinating anyone.

Later, perhaps. If it ever becomes necessary. For now, the thing to do is remain quiet and pretend we suspect nothing.

Poor Gretchko. He'll have to be silenced. And I'll have to get that damned Sword out of Stalin's office and off someplace where no one can be hurt by it. Or examine it.

28

Berlin, 28 April   Jarvick stood flat against the slim shelter of the doorway, breathing hard. Up the street the Sherman tank burned furiously. Nobody had gotten out. Some sonofabitch in one of those upstairs windows had hit it with a *panzerfaust* round. Now they would have to go up the street on their own, without armor support, and clean out the nest of snakes that was hiding in one of those buildings.

It looked like it wanted to rain, but Jarvick thought that the gray sky was more from the fires burning through the city and the thick clouds of plaster and concrete dust that choked the air. Berlin was being blasted apart, one building at a time.

Hollis came out from the interior of the building, clutching Kinder's Thompson submachine gun.

"Is he dead?" Jarvick asked.

Hollis's face was grimy, his eyes hollow with fatigue. The

grasshopper had turned into a grim, dust-caked dogface, just like all the others of the squad. They had been fighting street by street, building by building, for five days now. Patton's grand dash to Berlin had turned into a nightmare of grinding ceaseless hand-to-hand killing.

"The medics think he'll make it," Hollis said, his voice hoarse, "if they can get him back to the field station."

"Think the Krauts would shoot at a stretcher team?" Jarvick asked.

"Beats me."

Kaplan had been killed by a booby-trap mine yesterday. Loller had taken a beautiful flesh wound in the upper arm. Sanderson had disappeared during a firefight earlier that morning. Jarvick and Hollis were the only ones left of the original squad that had parachuted into Normandy less than a year earlier.

They saw DiMaggio coming up other side of the street, hugging the wall, rifle in both hands. He saw them and sprinted across the rubble-littered street. A machine gun chattered and bullets kicked up chips of paving. DiMaggio dived the last couple of yards into the doorway, knocking Hollis inside as Jarvick tried to melt himself into the stone doorway while bullets chipped away inches from his shoulder.

"Christ almighty!" DiMaggio spat concrete dust and sat up inside the safety of the doorway. "Why didn't you tell me?"

"What'd you expect?" Hollis yelled back. "Flowers?"

Jarvick could feel the sweat dripping down his back, beading his forehead and upper lip. But he had seen the gun flash when the Germans had opened up. He knew which window they were shooting from.

"Captain says we gotta take out that German pocket up

ahead. Tanks can't get through unless we clear out the Krauts from the upper stories."

"That's just great," Hollis griped. "Now we're protecting the fuckin' tanks."

"I saw their window," Jarvick said tightly. "If we had a bazooka we could knock 'em out from here."

Hollis shook his head. "Best we got is rifle grenades. We'll have to work in closer."

"Yeah."

Hollis called up what was left of the squad from the interior of the building. Reluctantly, warily, they steeled themselves to start up the street. Jarvick pointed out the window where he had seen the German gun flashes. The heavy-weapons men plastered it with automatic rifle fire as the others scurried, bent over double, a few doorways up. Then they covered the window with rifle and Tommy gun fire as the BAR men moved up.

It was methodical, almost mechanical. They had done it a hundred times before. It always worked. But it always cost.

One of the replacements, so new that Jarvick had not learned his name yet, fitted a grenade into the launching attachment on his rifle. The kid knelt behind the blackened hulk of the Sherman to take aim while the rest of the squad peppered the window and the ones next to it to keep the Krauts' heads down. The kid fired. A dull boom, then dirty gray smoke poured from the window.

"Got 'em, first shot!" the kid exulted.

Hollis gestured for three of the men to cross the street and advance to the doorway of that building. No one fired at them as they worked their way up the street on the far side, past the burning Sherman tank. Within minutes the whole squad had entered the building, through the shattered wooden front door, and cautiously nosed through its rooms. No one left alive. Up in the room they had shot at, four kids in German field gray coats lay sprawled in their own blood. One of them could not have been older than twelve.

Hollis gathered the squad together on the ground floor. "Okay, Joltin' Joe, go tell the captain that it's safe for the goddamned tanks to come up this far."

But before DiMaggio could get to the door they heard the clanking grumble of a tank out in the street. Coming the other way.

"Kraut tank?" Jarvick asked.

DiMaggio peered out the doorway. "Ain't one of ours, that's for sure."

Automatically the men checked out their grenades. They had nothing heavier.

"Christ, I didn't think the Krauts had any armor left," Hollis muttered as he stuck his head out the doorway.

The tank was low and wide and painted a light brown. A huge cannon poked out from its turret. And there was a red star painted on its front.

"Hey! I think they're Russians!"

The tank stopped half a block up the street, its gun pointing at the burning Sherman. The turret hatch popped open and a man in an odd-looking steel helmet raised his head cautiously.

"Amerikanski?" he called out, in a high tenor voice.

Hollis and DiMaggio stepped out onto the pockmarked street. A ray of sunshine broke through the smoke as they raised their hands and waved.

"Amerikanski!" Hollis yelled, his voice cracking. "You guys Russians?"

Jarvick came out beside them. "Tovarish!" he hollered. The one word of Russian he knew.

"Tovarish!" the Russian called back. From behind the tank came a full squad of soldiers armed with submachine guns, all yelling "Tovarish" and practically dancing up the street toward the Americans.

From his position on the rooftop across the street, fifteen-year-old Oswald Kaltenbrunner tried to ignore the pain in his legs as he listened to the invaders shouting at each other. He had lost a lot of blood, but he still had the sniper's rifle that the group leader had entrusted to him.

Dragging himself to the edge of the roof, he looked down to see the barbarian Russians and mongrel Americans embracing each other, shouting and hooting like the pack of wild animals they were. Oswald checked the rifle's magazine. He had only one bullet left. I will put it to good use, he told himself.

Down on the street, three stories below, the invaders were prancing with glee. Oswald pressed his eyes against the telescope sight and tried to keep his hands from shaking. It was not fear, he knew; it was fatigue, shock from loss of blood, pain from the wounds in his legs.

One of the Russians. Their officer. Oswald had memorized Russian insignia and rank markings. There. A swine of a captain. Probably the commander of several tanks. He sighted carefully, trying to keep the crosshairs of the telescope squarely between the broad shoulders of the Communist pig. His hands trembled so much that it was difficult. The rifle was heavy and he was utterly exhausted.

Jarvick saw the captain grinning at him and extending his hand. He took the Russian's hand in his own and said, "Are we glad to see you!"

"Da," said the captain. "Tovarish. Da."

Hollis came up and pounded the Russian on the shoulder. "Got any vodka?" He laughed.

The bullet missed the captain's shoulder by a centimeter

and smashed into Hollis' chest, knocking him backward off his feet. He felt nothing as he saw the building tilt crazily and then the gray smoky sky was all he could see. He could not move, but he heard gunfire and men swearing in two languages. Then the *pow* sound of a tank cannon and an immediate huge crumbling roar of an explosion. Black smoke drifted across the sky; rubble pelted down.

He saw faces hovering over him, blurry, out of focus, growing dim. One of them might have been Jarvick, looking sick and sorrowful.

"Not you," Jarvick said, breaking into tears. "Not you, buddy."

"Jesus, I think he's dead." Those were the last words Hollis heard.

The bunker was filled with fumes, a hazy drifting cloud of dust shaken loose by the ceaseless artillery pounding that had been going on for more than twelve hours up on the surface. Even this deep underground the rumble and thunder of the exploding shells pervaded everywhere, like the thudding of a heart convulsed by fear.

To Martin Bormann it seemed almost like a mystical scene from the *Götterdämmerung,* with a magical mist rising from the sacred river. But no, it was the dry chalky dust from the concrete slabs of the bunker. How long before even these thick reinforced walls and ceilings are smashed through? How long before the Russians and Americans shoot their way down here?

Hitler had not come out of his bedroom all day. He had screamed at Heinrici and the others for hours last night as he moved pins and flags representing long-destroyed battalions across his tabletop map of the city. He called the soldiers up above weaklings and cowards, even accused

Heinrici and his staff of deliberately throwing the battle away to the Russians and Americans. Tough old Heinrici was shaken; once Hitler had stormed off to his room it had taken Bormann a half-hour to convince the general that he had not taken the Führer's tirade literally.

"Have no fear that you will be shot by an SS bullet," Bormann had told him.

Heinrici had taken the hint. "No hand will strike me down," he had said, raising his own right fist, "except this one."

Now Bormann paced the length of the situation room alone. The relief map on the table was forgotten. He had sent all the others away, their faces white with fear and the knowledge of imminent death. He had a duty to perform, an obligation. How long should he wait?

The door at the far end of the long narrow room was opened by the guards stationed on its other side. An SS captain entered, strode up to Bormann, clicked his heels and saluted.

"Heil Hitler!"

Bormann flapped his hand in return. "What is the situation up there?"

The captain's face was blackened with smoke and grime, his uniform caked with gray dust and splotches of brown mud. But beneath the signs of battle his handsome Aryan face was set with determination. A true Hitler youth, fearless, actually delighting in the carnage of battle.

"The Russians and Americans have united. The city is almost entirely in their hands. Only the chancellery above us is still held by our men. They are fighting to the death."

Bormann ran a hand across his stubbly jaw. He had deliberately refrained from shaving for the past two days. His last hope had been that the Bolsheviks and the Americans would somehow turn on each other. Now he saw that he had been clutching foolishly at a straw. Time for his final plan.

"Captain, I want you to shower and get into a clean uniform. Quickly. Then I have a vital task for you to perform."

Bormann would be getting into another uniform, too. The field gray uniform of a plain soldier of the Wehrmacht. He stood a better chance of escaping this death trap as an ordinary soldier than as the infamous Martin Bormann.

"Don't shoot at any tanks," said the battalion commander. "Any tanks you see, they're either ours or Russians."

Staff Sergeant Al Rosenberg heard the order in his helmet earphones. His Sherman tank was buttoned up tight, pushing through a makeshift barricade of loose cobblestones and what looked like old furniture. The Krauts had put it up to block the broad avenue but the junk was no match for a Sherman.

Through the narrow viewing slit of his tank's turret Rosenberg saw an old bedspring rear up in front of the Sherman and then disappear beneath its treads. Nobody firing at them. Nobody in sight.

"Look out for mines," he said into his intercom microphone. The deafening roar of the diesel engine made ordinary conversation impossible; even shouting at the top of his lungs sometimes did not get down to the driver sitting just a few feet below him. Rosenberg remembered that when he had started training, a million years ago, tank commanders instructed their drivers by nudging them on the shoulders with their boots. The intercom radio was a helluva lot better, Rosenberg thought.

The hot burning anger he had felt a week ago no longer blazed inside him. The Germans were no longer tamely surrendering; they were fighting here in Berlin, fighting hard, and fear was what churned in his guts now. Still, underneath it all he still saw those haunted faces of the concentration camp prisoners, still felt a simmering hatred for each and every German in the world.

The rubble-strewn avenue opened onto a wide plaza. Most of the buildings around its perimeter were smoking, shell-pocked. Straight ahead was a huge building fronted by a wide stone stairway. Rosenberg could see gun flashes coming from the darkness behind the pillars at the top of the stairs.

"That's the chancellery! Right in front of us!" the battalion commander sounded excited.

There were little knots of infantrymen huddled here and there on the plaza, kneeling behind piles of rubble, crouched in shallow shell craters, even sprawled prone on the pavement. They were all firing into the chancellery building.

"Be careful not to hit any Russians," Rosenberg heard in his helmet earphones. "They'll be in brown coats. The Krauts are in gray."

Fashion report, Rosenberg thought.

"Stop here," ordered the battalion commander. "Fire at will on the chancellery building. Into the portico area at the top of the stairs."

Hitler's under there, Rosenberg thought as he turned the turret slightly and leveled the 75 millimeter cannon at the gun flashes. Beside him, his loader, a blond beardless kid named Jimmy, shoved a shell into the gun's breech and slammed it shut, then banged him on the shoulder.

Rosenberg pulled the trigger. The noise jolted him the way it always did and the turret filled with smoke. But we're not gonna pop the hatch to clear the fumes. Not now. Not yet.

"Come on, Jimmy," he shouted at his loader. "Speed i up."

Jimmy's face was streaming sweat. He nodded sullenly closed the breech and punched Rosenberg's shoulder harder than usual. Rosenberg fired again. And again. The top of the chancellery steps were lost in smoke and dust bu' all the tanks kept on pumping shells into the area.

"Come on!" Rosenberg shouted again. "More!"

"There ain't no more," Jimmy yelled back.

"We're out?" Rosenberg twisted around in his seat and saw nothing but empty racks.

"Not a shell left. We're done."

"The hell we are! Mickey!" he called down to the driver "put 'er in gear and move 'er straight ahead!"

"Are you crazy?" He could hear Mickey's high-pitched voice even without the intercom. "The rest of the battal ion's still pumpin' shells up there!"

"Do it, goddammit!" Rosenberg bellowed. "Do it!"

The tank lurched forward, slowly. The rest of 'em will run out of ammo just like we did, Rosenberg told himself. No sense letting the Krauts reorganize themselves. Hit 'em *now* before they can recover from the shelling.

"Rosenberg!" his earphones erupted. "What the fuck do you think you're doing?"

"Sir? Repeat please. I've got a lot of static here. Can' hear you."

"Get back! Stop! That's an order, Rosenberg!"

"Can't hear you, sir. Radio's on the fritz, I think."

"Goddammit, cease firing. Cease firing! Move forward, everybody. Move it up!"

Kendall Jarvick had been waiting out the tank barrage from behind a house-sized chunk of masonry that had been blasted from one of the buildings on the side of the plaza. He and DiMaggio had hunkered down when the Germans side the chancellery building began spraying the open laza with heavy machine-gun fire. Then the tanks had ome up and plastered the Krauts but good.

"About time the tanks did something for us," Joltin' Joe aid. Jarvick noted that the kid had become a typically ynical veteran in just a few days of hard fighting.

He heard machine-gun fire, but the lighter kind of noise hat American .50-calibers make. Peeking cautiously from he stone they were behind, Jarvick saw that a couple of the anks were peppering the chancellery roof line. That'll keep heir heads down, he said to himself, if any Krauts are still p there.

He thought about Hollis as the machine guns chattered nd the tank shells whistled past and exploded on the chan-ellery building. The last man in the squad he would expect o get it. There's no rhyme or reason to this killing. Grass-opper or ant or whatever, it catches up to you sooner or ater.

"Hey, they're goin' in!" DiMaggio said.

Jarvick looked up. The shelling had stopped and the anks were pushing through the rubble and around the ockets of infantry—some of them Russians—and heading traight for the broad stairway of the chancellery building. Io firing from the building. Nothing but smoke drifting rom the shattered remains of the facade up at the top of the teps.

One tank was in the lead, churning across the plaza like n eager St. Bernard. It came clanking and clamoring past he spot where they were crouching. Jarvick moved out ehind the tank, Tommy gun clutched in both hands. Di-Maggio hesitated only a fraction of a second, then stepped ut beside him. Both men bent over slightly and stayed ehind the tank's massive bulk.

Looking over his shoulder, Jarvick saw the other tanks

rumbling behind them. Soldiers climbed out of their holes and followed, just as he and Joltin' Joe were doing.

We're going to be the first ones inside the chancellery, Jarvick suddenly realized. For a moment he felt stunned. Then he told himself, You've got to see everything, remember everything. This is history being made, mister, and you're right here on the spot. It's a newspaperman's dream.

A heavy machine gun stuttered at them. Jarvick winced and ducked lower behind the advancing tank. Just don't get yourself killed, he said to himself as he slapped a fresh ammo magazine into his Thompson. That's the most important thing of all, don't get yourself killed.

29

Berlin, 28 April   Hitler was sitting in his study, attended by
no one except his bride, Eva Braun. They
had married that morning; Goebbels had performed the
brief, plain ceremony. Then Goebbels had bid his Führer a
tearful farewell and led his wife and five children to their
quarters. Fifteen minutes later one of the SS guards announced that they were all dead.

Eva sat in the corner of the small sofa, feet tucked up
under her like a little girl, hands pressed to her ears. Far
above them the bombardment was incessant, its once-
muted roar now a steady pounding thunder that could no
longer be ignored.

"If only they would stop, even for one minute," she said.

Hitler was staring off into space, unresponsive, lost to
her. On the end table beside his armchair was a bottle of
pills, a pitcher of water with two glasses, and a Luger auto-

matic pistol. Yet his hands remained in his lap, twitching slightly.

"The German people deserve this fate," Hitler said in a low trembling voice. "If they have not the courage and the will to triumph then they deserve to be driven into the mud and dust, exterminated once and for all. I could have led them to greatness, but they were not strong enough to follow me. Now they will all die."

Eva got up from the sofa and went to her husband. Kneeling before him, she put her head on his lap.

"I am dying now," she said softly.

He seemed to stir. Blinking, as if seeing her for the first time, he asked, "Dying?"

"The doctor gave me something to put in my tea. I knew this was our last day together, dear."

Hitler gazed down at her. "Dying?"

"We agreed, remember? I have taken the poison, just as you said I should. It is painless. It puts you to sleep, and then you don't wake up."

Her eyes closed. She seemed to be already asleep at his feet, her head on his thighs.

There was a tap on the door. Hitler did not answer, but the door opened anyway. A tall handsome blond SS captain stepped in, his uniform immaculate, the chiseled features of his face grave and somber.

"Listen," Hitler said to the captain.

The thundering up above had stopped. The captain turned his face toward the ceiling. It was quiet up there.

"They've stopped," said the captain.

"We've driven them away!"

The captain shook his head sadly. "No, my Führer. They have stopped the bombardment because their troops are now assaulting our final positions. This bunker will be over-run in another few minutes. Half an hour, at most."

"We've driven them away, I tell you!" Hitler tried to shout out the words, but his voice broke.

The captain took his pistol from the gleaming holster at his hip.

"What are you doing?" Hitler demanded.

"My duty, sir."

"No! I command you—"

"Herr Bormann's orders, my Führer."

Hitler tried to struggle to his feet, but Eva's dead weight on his legs defeated him. The captain fired one shot, point-blank.

"Sir, it's *dangerous* up there!"

Patton snorted at his aide. "I haven't come this goddam far to sit on my ass in the rear. Get this jeep going!" he ordered his driver. "Follow those tanks."

The young captain grabbed both sides of the hard rear bench as the driver dug in the clutch and lurched the jeep down the rubble-covered street. He was distinctly unhappy. The general might want to be a bigshot hero, all the captain wanted to do was to live out this war and get home all in one piece.

Sitting stiffly in the right-hand seat, Patton grumbled to himself about the quality of the officers they were turning out these days. Had to put that other punk kid into the line; make a man of him. Now they send me a college boy still wet behind the ears.

They heard the sound of shelling up ahead, the *crack* of tank guns immediately followed by the *crump* of explosions and the rumble of masonry crumbling.

"They must be right at the chancellery building!" Patton yelled exultantly over the noise and the wind as the jeep turned a corner and came out on a broad avenue. There had been a barricade here, but the tanks had obviously smashed through it. The driver downshifted and slowed the jeep to a crawl.

"What's the matter, sergeant?" Patton groused.

"Mines, sir. Don't want to hit a mine."

"Bullshit! The Krauts have been too busy retreating to lay mines here."

"General, sir, they've had damn near six years to lay mines here."

Patton glowered at his driver but said nothing more. The sergeant was a tough old noncom, regular Army, who had been driving Patton since the first landings in Morocco. He could by a tyrant in his way, as all good noncoms were, but his first thought was always to take the best of care of his general.

By the time they reached the chancellery plaza the shelling had stopped. Patton saw his Shermans advancing right up to the chancellery steps. One of them even started clawing its way up the steps, clanking right up to the top, spraying machine-gun fire into the smoking darkness of the portico.

"That boy's got guts!" the general yelled, standing in the jeep.

The other tanks stopped at the bottom of the stairs. Bent figures of infantrymen climbed the steps slowly, warily. Most of them were Americans. Patton beamed at them.

Inside his Sherman, Al Rosenberg swung the turret back and forth. Spent shell casings from his machine gun clattered around his feet. Even the trigger of the gun felt hot to his touch. On the other side of the seventy-five's breech, Jimmy was trying to wave away the acrid fumes.

It was dark and smoky up at the top of the stairs. Rosenberg could see nothing except dead German soldiers, blasted chunks of rubble, and more dead Germans. Good. Infantry dogfaces came sifting through the smoke, rifles and carbines held out in front of them, cautiously looking every which way as they edged deeper into the shadows. One of them held a Tommy gun, Rosenberg saw.

He unlatched the hatch at the turret's top, then took the carbine from its clip alongside the empty ammo rack.

"Whattarya doin'?" Jimmy asked.

"Come on," Rosenberg said, clambering up through the hatch. "Let's go see Adolph."

Jimmy blinked, but unclipped the carbine on his side of the turret.

"Cut the engine and stay tight, Mickey," Rosenberg hollered down to the tank driver.

"Don't worry, I ain't movin'," Mickey replied fervently.

Rosenberg and Jimmy fell in beside the guy with the Tommy gun. "Hundred and first airborne, huh?" Rosenberg said.

"That's right," answered Jarvick.

They pushed through the shattered doors of the chancellery and entered the building. Soldiers were fanning out across a huge marble-floored area with a ceiling so high it was lost in the smoke and dust.

"Nice place," said DiMaggio tightly.

"They did all right for themselves," Rosenberg said.

A burst of gunfire from off to their right. Then the sullen thud of a grenade and someone screaming in bloody agony.

"Got a couple more of the bastards," Rosenberg muttered.

"Or they got a couple of our guys," said Jarvick.

It took nearly an hour for them to find the stairs that led down to the bunker. They heard a few more brief firefights, but most of the time it was eerily quiet except for the glass and rubble crunching beneath their boots. Smoke drifted everywhere. The men spoke in hushed monosyllables.

They reached the bottom of the stairs and stepped into a

large, low-ceilinged room with a big map of the city spread out on a couple of saw horses. Jarvick counted seven dead bodies, all in black SS uniforms.

"This is his bunker, huh?" Rosenberg asked one of the soldiers who had come down before them.

"This is it."

"Where is the sonofabitch?"

Before he could answer they heard something that prickled the hair on the backs of their necks. Men singing. Their voices muffled, but getting louder. Singing!

> *Deutschland, Deutschland über Alles,*
> *über Alles in der Welt . . .*

"What the hell?"

"Where's it coming from?"

> *Wenn es stets zu Schutz and Trutz*
> *bruderlich . . .*

"It's comin' closer."

Suddenly a door across the room burst open and black-uniformed SS men poured through, firing machine pistols and automatic rifles. Jarvick flopped on his belly, spraying them with his submachine gun as he fell. Rosenberg dived under the sawhorse-supported map table. Pure hell erupted in the bunker room, gunfire flashing and bullets whining off the concrete walls and men screaming, cursing.

It was all over in less than half a minute. Rosenberg smelled blood and cordite. His hands were locked on his carbine, gripping it so tightly that his fingers hurt. Yet he had not fired a shot. Redfaced with shame and guilt, he crawled out from under the table and got shakily to his feet.

All the Krauts lay sprawled on the concrete, dead. Jarvick was sitting on the floor, holding his bleeding leg and rocking back and forth, white-lipped with pain. Jimmy lay beside him, his face staring sightlessly at the ceiling. Rosenberg threw up.

Within minutes the medics were in, helping the wounded. Jarvick grinned painfully as two husky infantrymen lifted him tenderly to his feet, his right thigh tightly tourniqueted. They started walking him out toward the stairs. And sunlight. And home.

I did it, Jarvick said to himself, half delirious with the sudden knowledge that his fighting was over. The million-dollar wound. I got it. They'll send me home now. I'm out of it.

He did not think about history any more, or even about simple journalism. All he thought about was getting home and back to his wife. Even if they have to take the leg off, he told himself, I'm going to live. I'm going to live.

Rosenberg watched the men take out the wounded. Others collected the dogtags of the dead. They left the Germans alone. He stared down at Jimmy's dead body. It's my fault, he groaned to himself. I made him come down here. And then I didn't even fire a fucking goddamned shot.

"Where's Hitler?" he asked one of the soldiers. "I thought he was supposed to be down in here."

"He is," said a corporal.

"Where?"

The soldier nodded toward one of the doors. So this is the face of victory, Rosenberg thought. The corporal did not look victorious. Not glad or even relieved that the fighting was at last finished. He just looked tired, drained, an old man in his early twenties who had already seen a lifetime of killing.

Rosenberg pushed past him and rushed to the open doorway. A lieutenant stood in the far corner of the little room, poking through the bottles and vials on the table there.

Adolph Hitler sat on an easy chair, arms hanging nearly to the floor, head thrown back, mouth open in a soundless "oh," a neat nine-millimeter bullet hole in the center of his forehead. A woman's body lay on the floor a few feet away, her lips the same color as the light blue dress she wore, her eyes closed. Someone had folded her arms reverently across her chest. Rosenberg saw that the floor behind Hitler's chair was spattered with drying blood and gray bits of brain and bone.

"He's already dead," Rosenberg said.

"Yeah," said the lieutenant from across the room. "Looks like one of his own men shot him."

Rosenberg felt the bile rising in his throat again. He swallowed it down, though, burning acid inside him. That's Adolph Hitler, he said to himself, staring at the dead body. That's the bastard who started this war and killed every Jew he could get his hands on. Wordlessly he unslung the carbine from his shoulder, the carbine he had not used in the firefight where Jimmy got killed. He cocked it with a loud mechanical *click*.

The lieutenant had time enough to say, "Hey soldier, what do you think you're—"

"Stinking sonofabitch!" Rosenberg screamed. He fired the whole clip into Hitler, the blast of the carbine echoing off the concrete walls, cordite smell burning in his nostrils. The lieutenant dived for the floor. Hitler's body jounced and twisted, arms flailing.

The carbine ran out of bullets. Rosenberg's ears rang in the sudden silence.

"Goddammit, sergeant, you'll get a court martial for that!" the lieutenant yelled, climbing to his feet.

Rosenberg threw the empty carbine to the floor. "The sonofabitch oughtta be chopped up into dog meat," he shouted. "He oughtta be . . ." But his voice broke and he buried his face in his hands, sobbing uncontrollably.

"Ten-*hut!*"

The lieutenant snapped to attention. Rosenberg stood

alf bent over in front of Hitler, crying. General Patton trode into the room, growling, "What in hell was that ring . . ."

Patton's voice trailed off. His baggy eyes went from Hitler's riddled body to Rosenberg's carbine at his feet, still smoking. Then he stepped over to Rosenberg and gently pried his hands away from his tear-streaked face.

General Patton looked into Rosenberg's eyes for a long moment.

"He shot up the corpse, sir!" yelped the lieutenant. "He came in here and emptied the whole clip into Hitler's body!"

Patton smiled grimly. "Can't say I blame you, son," he said softly. "I would've done the same thing myself. Sorry you beat me to it."

"But general—"

"Get this man to the medics," Patton snapped. "And haul this piece of garbage out of here. I guess they'll want to stuff him and exhibit him at the Smithsonian or something like that."

t was more than an hour later that Patton emerged from the chancellery building. The plaza was swarming with troops, Americans and Russians. At the sight of his three-starred helmet and ivory-handled pistols, the GIs burst into a prolonged cheer. Patton looked surprised at first, then grinned and waved his hands over his head.

"We did it!" he yelled. "The paperhanging sonofabitch is stone cold dead!"

The cheering went on and on. A Russian jeep came bouncing up the steps and two officers got out to shake Patton's hand. One of them spoke English:

"General Patton, sir, may I introduce Field Marshal Georgi Konstantinovitch Zhukov."

Patton saw a short, solidly built man with a hard-bitten

expression on his face. But his eyes were bright clear blue. He said something in Russian and the translator said:

"Marshal Zhukov says he congratulates the general who captured Berlin."

Patton uncharacteristically blushed. "Tell him that we did it together."

Zhukov's hard blunt face broke into a big grin and he stuck out his hand. Patton took it and the soldiers all around them cheered again.

"Tonight we celebrate," said the translator. "Marshal Zhukov wishes you to be his guest at dinner."

"No," Patton said. "He's got to be my guest tonight. I insist."

Zhukov's eyes flashed when the translator explained, but then he nodded and said simply, "Da."

The two men shook hands again and parted. Patton walked down the steps, still cheered by his men, and climbed into his jeep, muttering, "Goddam commie general thinks he's going to upstage me, does he?"

His sergeant driver laughed, his captain aide looked worried. They started off across the plaza.

"We've got to find a good place to have a celebration dinner," Patton said to the captain. "I just invited Zhukov to dine with us tonight."

"Yessir. I'll take care of it."

"Good. Do that."

"Then it's done, sir?" the sergeant asked, over the wind rushing past as they drove through the rubble in the streets. "Hitler's dead and the war's finished?"

"The sonofabitch is dead all right. Now the politicians can make it all official and sign a cease-fire."

"You did it, sir," said the sergeant, grinning hugely. "You took Berlin."

"Damn right. This is the best day of my life!"

They bounced across a section of the street where the paving stones had been pulled up to make a barricade. A sixteen-year-old Hitler Youth had planted a land mine in the unpaved dirt and the jeep drove over it. The mine exploded, knocking the left front wheel off the jeep and hurling fragments into the driver's abdomen and chest, killing him instantly. The captain was lifted off the back seat several inches and slammed down hard again, fracturing his coccyx. Patton was thrown over the windscreen and hood, his helmet flying. The general landed on his back, his spine broken, as the jeep plowed to a halt inches from his bare head.

Dazed, the captain struggled out of the jeep, shocked at the pain in his legs and back. He staggered to his general and collapsed beside him.

"Christ, what a way to die," Patton mumbled.

"I'll get the medics," said the captain, breathless with shock as he tried to struggle to his feet.

"Yeah. Yeah. But I got Berlin, didn't I? He let me take Berlin first."

And General George S. Patton was suddenly and ingloriously dead.

30

London, 30 April   Winston Churchill sat in his above-
ground office at 10 Downing Street, look-
ing out at the rain. It was a gray windswept day outside, a
nearly perfect match to his inner mood. He should feel
triumphant, joyous, he told himself. Yet he felt nothing but
grim unease.

"Mr. Philby, Prime Minister," said his secretary, from
the door.

Philby had sent a handwritten request for a personal
meeting with the Prime Minister. It said simply, *Must speak
to you privately about the Sword. Philby.* Instantly alarmed,
Churchill had swiftly agreed to meet with the young man
from SIS.

Churchill nodded and reached for a cigar from the massive humidor on his desk. "Send him in."

Kim Philby looked even less at ease than Churchill felt.
Yet there was a defiant glare in his eye. Churchill had seen

that burning expression many years before, in Kilby's father. Jack Philby had been one of those madmen who hated the very Establishment that had given him a world of privilege and protection.

Rising from behind his desk as the young man crossed toward him, Churchill indicated the leather wing chairs by the window.

"Let's sit here," he said, forcing a smile. "I have been living below ground like a mole for so long that even a rainy day looks glorious to me."

Philby nodded tightly and took one of the chairs. As Churchill sat and puffed his cigar alight, Philby pulled a silver cigarette case from his jacket.

"I haven't seen you in several years, Kim. Not since you started with the Intelligence Service. How have you been?"

"Rather well, Winston," said Philby, with none of the respect that a young man should show to his Prime Minister. But then this young man had known Churchill since childhood.

Churchill puffed on his cigar and considered ringing for sherry or perhaps something stronger as he watched Philby light his cigarette with an engraved silver Dunhill. The driving rain peppered the window.

"I suppose I should congratulate you," Philby said, clicking the lighter shut. "On winning the war and all that."

Churchill smiled warily. "The press has called me the British lion. But in reality, it was the British people who have been the lion. I was merely in a position to give the lion's roar."

"Very pretty," said Philby. "Do you plan to use that in a speech?"

"When the time comes," Churchill said. "What is it that you wanted to see me about?"

"Berlin."

"Berlin? Don't tell me you want to be posted there?"

"Not at all. But it wasn't until the Yanks took all the glory for capturing Berlin that I realized how truly clever you've been. About the Sword of Stalingrad, I mean."

Churchill glowered at him. "What about the Sword of Stalingrad?"

"I've put together the whole scheme, Winston: the plutonium, the Sword, Stalin's sudden demise, and finally your victory in Berlin."

"The late and very much lamented General Patton took Berlin," Churchill said. "With some help from the Russians."

"Yes, but Stalin isn't around any more, is he? His untimely death wasn't terribly untimely at all, was it? He died and the Russian advance on Berlin stalled just long enough for Patton to dash to the city and claim the victory."

"We were very fortunate, although certainly Monty doesn't see it that way. Odd thing, though," Churchill added before Philby could reply, "with Patton getting himself killed, Monty finds it impossible to criticize him or Eisenhower. The fortunes of war can be exceeding strange, can't they?"

"You assassinated the leader of our most powerful ally," Philby said, his voice ringing with bitterness.

Churchill said nothing for a long moment. Then, removing the cigar from his mouth, he leaned toward the young man and said slowly, "That is a very large accusation, Kim. Have you any proof to back it up?"

"None whatsoever."

Churchill spread his hands in a gesture of vindication. "Then where are you?"

"The Russians could examine the Sword, you know."

"Only if someone prodded them to it."

"I could."

"Are you so convinced of your idea that you would risk a charge of treason?"

Philby's brows arched and he fell silent. He did not tell his Prime Minister that he had already tried his utmost to make the Russians examine the possibilities he suspected and failed to get any response at all from his contacts in Moscow. Indeed, one of them seemed to have vanished from the Earth altogether.

Churchill got to his feet. "Let me paint you a picture, young Kim. A picture such as the kind your father Jack would have appreciated."

"Really?"

"Yes, of course. Your father would have liked to have lived to see this day. The British Empire is finished as a world power. And I am finished as a politician."

"Now really, Winston," said Philby sarcastically.

Pacing slowly across the room, with Philby turning in his chair to follow, Churchill explained, "This war has exhausted Britain. The Yanks and the Russians are the two Great Powers now. Britain is a distinctly secondary figure on the world stage. Our only role will be as a sort of senior adviser to the Americans—who frankly need all the good advice they can get."

Despite himself, Philby grinned at that.

"Imagine what the world would be like if Stalin were still alive and the Russians alone had taken Berlin. Stalin would turn all of Eastern Europe into a Soviet vassal state. But he would never be satisfied with that. Like Ivan the Terrible and all those other paranoids who have haunted the Kremlin, he would feel unsafe until he had taken the rest of Europe into his grasp. Like Hitler, he would then want to leap across the Channel and place us in his thrall. Sooner or later the Americans—no matter how reluctant they might be—would wake up and go to war against Stalin."

Philby gasped, "With atomic bombs."

"You know about that, do you?" Churchill cocked an eye at the young man. "How long do you think it would be before Stalin built such bombs of his own?"

"Not long. A few years, at most."

"Then we should see a world conflict that would reduce all of civilization to ashes. Is that what you want?"

Regaining some of his composure, Philby said, "But that isn't going to happen now, is it? Stalin is dead and the new Soviet leadership is less likely to be as—how did you put it—as *paranoid* as Stalin was. Besides, the Americans are in Berlin. And most of Austria, as well as a good slice of Czechoslovakia, too."

Churchill nodded. "Yes. If they play their cards correctly the Yanks will be masters of the world. We must help them to carry that burden."

"Must we?" Philby's voice dripped acid.

"Of course we must. Think of it: America will have the atomic bomb very shortly. Japan will be finished within the year, I'm certain. When the shooting finally stops, America will be the most powerful nation in the history of the world. Her navies rule all the saltwater on Earth. Her armies have triumphed in Europe and the Far East. And she will have sole possession of the atomic bomb. It will be—to use Henry Luce's grandiose expression—the American century. A world of peace and order, enforced by American power."

"With British guidance."

"If we are clever enough to guide them wisely."

"It sounds horrible to me," said Philby.

Churchill took a puff of his cigar. "It is not exactly what I would have wanted, either. But it will be the best we can hope for. America will have to keep the Russians in their place while we rebuild Europe."

"Ghastly."

"Would you rather be facing Stalin and his hordes across the Channel?"

"I don't regard the triumph of socialism as anathema, Winston, the way you do."

"The triumph of Stalin would be as bad as the triumph of Hitler. Worse, no doubt."

"And that is why you had Stalin assassinated, is it?"

Churchill studied his half-spent cigar, pondering the young man's question for a long silent moment. Then, "With the inevitable end of Hitler and his odious crew, it seemed to me that the common danger which had united our great alliance would quickly vanish. The Soviet menace would replace the Nazi foe. But no comradeship against the Soviets existed as yet. The Americans had not yet awakened to the new facts of the situation. How could we then reach that final settlement in Europe which alone could reward the toils and sufferings of our struggle?"

Philby's eyes glittered with self-satisfaction. "But all that could be changed if Stalin were removed from the scene."

"As you said, his death was not untimely."

Philby fell silent for several moments. Then he asked, "What was that you said about your being finished as a politician?"

"The foundations of national unity upon which our wartime government has stood so firmly will also soon be gone. Our strength will be dissipated in party politics and bickering."

"You mean you won't be able to rule with an absolute hand as you have for the past five years."

Shrugging, "The war cabinet will resign within a month or so. We shall have the first general election since before the war. I will be turned out of office, I'm quite sure. Democracies usually reward their war leaders with a boot in the rear as soon as the shooting stops."

"What will you do?"

"Write books, I suppose. Offer my opinions on as wide a world stage as I can manage. I will remain in the Commons, of course. I shall always remain in the Commons."

"You'll be knighted, certainly."

"I would rather remain Prime Minister and help lead this nation through the difficult times that lie ahead."

"You did assassinate Stalin, didn't you?" Philby asked suddenly, like a prosecuting attorney trying to startle a confession out of a witness.

"And you are a Soviet spy, aren't you?" Churchill countered.

Philby gasped.

Churchill returned to his wing chair and leaned earnestly toward the young man. "It doesn't matter, Kim. None of it matters, except to protect and preserve this marvelous civilization our fathers have bequeathed us. Hitler nearly destroyed it, but we have come through—battered, ruined financially, but still alive. Democracy has survived. Stalin would have been the final straw, he would have brought it all down on our heads. You can see that, can't you?"

"All I see is that you murdered the leader of our most powerful ally," Philby said. "In your blind hatred and fear of socialism you committed cold-blooded deliberate murder."

"What you fail to see is that Stalin's murderous ambitions had nothing to do with socialism or communism or any other *ism* except the expansion of Russian power. He was not an idealogue; he was a power-mad maniac."

"And thus had to be stopped, because he threatened British power."

"No," said Churchill firmly. "Because he threatened *American* power. They would fight for global supremacy with atomic bombs, sooner or later. That is what I sought to prevent."

Philby shook his head stubbornly.

Churchill sank back in his chair as if suddenly exhausted by the effort of justifying himself to this young upstart. Then he added, "Besides, socialism is going to triumph right here in Britain, very shortly. Not Stalin's sort of dictatorial tyranny, but it will be disastrous enough, believe me."

"Do you really think that Labour will win the election?"

Sourly, Churchill replied, "I do. Attlee and Bevin and that ilk. They will turn to socialism as hard as the electorate will allow them to."

"Then I shall vote for them."

"God save the King," Churchill muttered.

Philby rose to his feet. "Thank you for your time, Prime Minister."

Getting up from his chair again, Churchill offered his hand to the young man. "Do you know, Kim, I believe that you are an even stranger duck than your father."

That brought a genuine smile to Philby's face. He shook Churchill's hand and left the office.

"A Russian spy," Churchill murmured to the empty office. Then he thought, *If I do anything to apprehend him, he'll start blubbering about the Sword of Stalingrad. Better to make certain that SIS puts him in the most innocuous post possible. Perhaps a transfer to Australia. Or better yet, Havana. He'll like it there; plenty of women and gambling and a fascist strongman named Batista for him to hate and plot against.*

Then he looked out at the rain-streaked window and remembered that he had better do whatever needed doing quickly. *I won't have that power much longer,* Churchill said to himself. I can only hope that Attlee will refuse to investigate Broadsword, should he ever be informed of it.

Washington, D.C., 30 April   It was a beautiful springtime afternoon. The drapes had been pulled aside to allow the sunshine through. Beyond the long windows of the Oval Office the azaleas were in full bloom and the dogwood trees made graceful arches of white and pink blossoms.

"So it's finished, then?" Harry Hopkins asked.

"Yes," said Roosevelt, from behind his broad cluttered desk. "Hermann Goering will sign the surrender papers tomorrow. All the fighting has stopped, except for a few die-hard fanatics here and there. By this time tomorrow even they will have laid down their arms."

The President could see that his old friend was fidgeting nervously in his chair, badly wanting a cigarette. But Roosevelt also knew that the smell of cigarette smoke would make *him* want one, too, and he had no intention of going back to that habit.

So he smiled broadly at Hopkins and suggested, "Harry, you should try chewing gum."

Hopkins started to frown at his boss, ended up grinning sheepishly. He did not look good: gray pallor, nervously thin. I've overworked him, Roosevelt thought. Overworked us all. Well, maybe now we can relax a little. Now that Hitler's finished we can concentrate on the Japs and end this war in another year or so.

"The Russians want to try Goering and all the other top Nazis as criminals," Hopkins said. "Molotov told me so."

The President nodded gravely. "After seeing the pictures of the death camps, I agree entirely."

"Do we have them all now?"

"All except Martin Bormann. Patton's boys caught

Himmler trying to pass himself off as a private. Once they realized who he was, he killed himself with poison: a cyanide capsule in his teeth, apparently."

"They'd better make sure Goering and the others don't do the same," Hopkins said.

"They are taking all the necessary precautions," said Roosevelt. "If I understand Goering correctly, he'll be more interested in posing as a great man than in committing suicide."

"How's Churchill feeling about all this?"

"I haven't spoken with Winston since yesterday. He's beginning to worry about the elections he promised to hold once the war with Germany was over."

"Surely he'll win any election hands down."

Roosevelt pivoted his wheelchair slightly to gaze out at the garden. A fat robin was hopping across the grass, looking for worms.

"I don't know about that, Harry. If we had an election here before the end of the year, would *I* be returned to office?"

He watched Hopkins out of the corner of his eye. His friend and confidant smiled at the question, then replied, "Franklin, you could be made king if you wanted to be."

Roosevelt threw his head back and laughed heartily. "I doubt that, Harry. I truly doubt it."

"But do you think Churchill is really in trouble? After all he's done?"

"Democracies often cast aside their leaders after a great crisis has been weathered. Lincoln got the best of it, you know, being assassinated right after he had won the Civil War."

"But who could replace Churchill?" Hopkins' voice was filled with troubled admiration.

Roosevelt turned back to face him directly. "It doesn't

much matter, Harry. Britain is finished as a great power. This war has exhausted her. It's up to us now, we are the most powerful nation on Earth. We and the Russians."

"There's still the Japs."

The President waved a hand in the air impatiently. "Japan is finished. The Japanese have tremendous courage, but their suicide attacks merely show how little they have left to fight with. No, Japan is finished. The Empire of the Rising Sun will never be a powerful nation again."

"But the Russians?"

"We have got to find a way to convince them that allowing free elections in Poland is in their own best interest. I've told Stettinius to make clear to them that we have not fought a war that began in Poland merely to see the Polish people fall under the rule of the Soviet Union. And the same goes for the other countries of Eastern Europe. You know, Harry, our troops now occupy a good part of Central Europe and I have no intention of pulling them out until we've settled this Polish question with Moscow."

"But the postwar zones of occupation were settled at Yalta," Hopkins said.

Roosevelt looked out at the garden again. "I don't think we should pull our troops out of the areas they've already conquered, do you?"

"Well, we agreed—"

"Those agreements were more theoretical than practical. I think we should renegotiate, don't you, Harry? How would Molotov and the others react to a new conference, here in Washington, perhaps? Under the auspices of the United Nations Organization?"

Hopkins sank back in his chair as if a six-hundred pound sack of cement had been dropped in his lap.

"It would be an excellent way to get the United Nations off to a flying start, wouldn't it?" Roosevelt enthused. "An

nternational conference to settle the boundaries of the new
Europe."

"Molotov won't like having it held here."

"But he'll come. He'll come. He'll have to come, if the others—Britain, France, China, the smaller nations—if they all agree to
meet here."

"Yes, I suppose he will have to come," Hopkins said
weakly.

"Good!" said Roosevelt. "Do you feel up to one more
trip to Moscow?"

"If you need me to, sure."

"That's fine, Harry. This will be the last time, I promise
you. I want you to break this idea to Molotov personally,
informally. Then we can get the State Department to handle
the formal arrangements."

"I see."

"Thank you, Harry. This will be the last time you have
to go to Moscow, I promise."

Hopkins grinned and got to his feet. He knew that
Roosevelt did not make promises easily. He also knew that
any promises the President made to his oldest and most
trusted assistant were nonenforceable.

Hopkins lit a cigarette the instant he stepped through the
door to the outer office. Henry Stimson was on his way in,
tall, spare, austere in his gray three-piece suit. Stimson
coughed and nodded by way of greeting.

The President gave Stimson his "I'm so delightfully
pleased that you could come see me" smile, wheeled around
from behind his desk and gestured the Secretary of War to
one of the couches by the empty fireplace.

"Sit down, Henry. Make yourself comfortable."

They chatted amiably for a few moments. Stimson respected Roosevelt more than any President he had worked
for, with the possible exception of his uncle Teddy. He knew

FDR well enough to realize that the trivial chitchat would end soon enough.

Finally the President said, "Henry, I would like you to bring me up to date on the Manhattan Project."

Stimson thought that Roosevelt sounded almost reluctant, as if he were facing a chore that was necessary but unwelcome. He replied, "I should ask Dr. Oppenheimer to fly in from New Mexico, then, and—"

"No, no, nothing so detailed or formal. I just want to know how the project is proceeding."

Fiddling with his watch chain, Stimson said, "Progress is good. They should be ready to test the bomb in a few months."

Roosevelt sat in silence for a few moments, his face somber.

"How should we use the bomb, Henry?" he asked. "What would be the best way to employ it?"

"Do you mean which Japanese cities should be targeted for attack?"

"No—although that's part of it, I suppose." The President hesitated, then said, "The Japanese are beaten. Our B-29s are burning out all of their major cities. It's only a matter of time until Japan starves and collapses. Do we have to blow up entire cities with the bomb, too?"

"The atomic bomb could convince them to surrender," Stimson said. "We wouldn't have to invade their home islands and incur all the casualties which would be involved."

"Yes, perhaps," said Roosevelt. "But what I'm wondering about is, how could we best employ the bomb to show the Russians how powerful it is? You see, Henry, it's not the Japanese we have to worry about now. It's the Russians. I want to make certain that they know we have this new eapon, that we will use it to enforce our policy decisions, nd—" the President leaned forward and tapped Stimson's nee to drive home his final point, "—we will not allow any ther nation to acquire atomic weaponry."

Stimson's face went white. He looked aghast. "My god, Ir. President! What you're proposing is American hegemny—a worldwide American empire!"

Roosevelt tried to smile but failed. Instead he looked orried, almost fearful. "Henry, once the Japanese finally ive up and the shooting stops, we will have the responsibily for leading the entire world. There is no blinking at that imple fact. You may not like it. To tell the truth, neither do . But our task does not end when the fighting stops. ather, it truly begins. It's much easier to fight a war than o produce a just and lasting peace after the war. But that our task now, our responsibility. There is no one else who an do it."

Stimson sat as if frozen, his face a grim mask.

"There is no one else except us, Henry," Roosevelt reeated. "We have got to show everyone, and especially the ussians, that we intend to lead the world into a just and asting peace."

"A *pax Americana,*" Stimson muttered.

"Exactly," said the President, with a tired almost sorrowul sigh. "We made a bad mistake after the last war and that ed to this one. I have no intention of allowing this nation o make that mistake again."

Stimson clearly did not like the idea, but just as clearly he ad no alternative to offer. He left the Oval Office looking ired and troubled.

Roosevelt sat in his wheelchair alone. This is what victory s, he told himself. Not glory, but responsibility. Not trimph but endless burdens. His head throbbed painfully.

Wheeling himself back toward his desk, he wondered if there might not be an old pack of cigarettes still hidden in one of its drawers.

Moscow, 30 April   Marshal Kliment Yefremovich Voroshilov, Inspector General of the Red Army, felt distinctly uneasy in the former office of Josef Stalin. It was like visiting a haunted house. Stalin had been such a powerful personality all through the Marshal's life that he more than half-expected the Man of Steel to come walking through the door angrily demanding to know what they were doing in his office.

For more than two weeks the office had been sealed. Ever since the fateful morning when the Great One had died, no one but his private secretary had been allowed inside. And even he, the private secretary, had died a few days later; some said he died of grief for his lost leader.

Voroshilov personally supervised the men who were clearing out Stalin's old office, carting the furnishings off to a museum that would be erected in the Great One's honor. Teams of soldiers in coveralls had already taken out the desk, the chairs, and Stalin's hidden dais. Now they were emptying the bookcases, stuffing the reports that had filled them into wooden crates, to be sent to the appropriate government libraries.

The word was that Molotov had wanted this office, but Khrushchev had beaten him to the punch and taken it for himself. Voroshilov shrugged. Such nonsense did not appeal to him at all.

He saw that one of the coverall-clad soldiers was reaching for the Sword of Stalingrad, the last ornament still hanging on the wall.

"Be careful with that," Voroshilov snapped. "It's going to the War Museum."

"Not to the Stalin Museum?" asked the captain who was checking off each item on his clipboard.

"No. To the War Museum. It was his personal wish," said Voroshilov.

Despite himself, Voroshilov edged slightly away as the soldiers removed the Sword from the wall and carried it outside the office. He remembered when he himself had been handed the Sword by Stalin, at Tehran, and had ignominiously dropped it. He had known that it was harmless at that point, and it should be harmless now. But still he edged away and glanced at the door, almost expecting to see the wrathful ghost of his former master pointing an accusing finger at him.

I'll have to get someone to remove the plutonium, someone I can trust. Then the Sword can remain on public display and the plutonium can be buried somewhere forever.

His normally dour face grew even more somber than usual. Yes, I will need a trustworthy man. He will be the last victim of Josef Stalin. The very last.

Author's Afterword

Although a work of fiction, this novel is based as solidly as possible on known historical data. Everything that happened in actual history prior to 1 April 1945 is assumed to be part of the background of this novel. From 1 April onward, however, events diverge in this alternate universe of the imagination.

For those readers who are not familiar with the history of our world, Winston Churchill did indeed present Josef Stalin with the Sword of Stalingrad at the Tehran Conference on 29 November 1943. It was not an assassination weapon. It now is on display in the War Museum in Moscow. Josef Stalin lived until 1953. Lavrentii Beria was shot soon after Stalin's death and Nikita Khrushchev eventually became the president of the Soviet Union and general secretary of the Soviet Communist Party.

Franklin Delano Roosevelt never gave up smoking. He died of a cerebral hemorrhage on 12 April 1945.

The Red Army captured Berlin in a fierce battle that raged from 16 April until 2 May 1945. Hitler committed suicide in his Berlin bunker on 30 April, ten days after his fifty-sixth birthday. The American and British armies stopped at the Elbe, for the most part, as Eisenhower had outlined in his memorandum of 28 March 1945. The Soviet Union occupied all of Eastern Europe and set up Communist regimes in Poland, Romania, Bulgaria, Albania, Hungary and Czechoslovakia. The ensuing Cold War between the East and West lasted until 1990.

Eisenhower was elected President of the United States in 1952. Patton died 21 December 1945 after being injured in an automobile accident near Mannheim, Germany. Captain Glenn Miller, director of the U.S. Air Forces band, disappeared on the flight of a light plane across the fogenshrouded English Channel 15 December 1944. Hermann Goering, found guilty of war crimes by the International Military Tribunal at Nuremberg, committed suicide. To this day no one knows how he got the poison with which he killed himself.

Klaus Fuchs continued to spy for the Soviet Union until 1947, when he was arrested. Convicted of espionage in 1950, he was sentenced to fourteen years in prison. He was released in 1959, his sentence shortened for good behavior. He immediately fled to East Germany, where he was made deputy director of the nuclear research institution and a member of the Central Committee of the East German Communist Party. He died 28 January 1988.

Kim Philby was never apprehended by British justice. He continued his espionage work until 1963 when, fearing arrest, he defected to the Soviet Union where he remained until his death on 11 May 1988.

Winston Churchill, turned out of office by the elections of July 1945, became Prime Minister once more in 1951. He ived to be 90 and was given a hero's funeral in London in 1965. Yuri Gagarin became the first man to fly in space when he orbited the Earth aboard the *Vostok 1* spacecraft 12 April 1961.

SCIENCE FICTION BY
BEN BOVA

☐ 53217-1   ASTRAL MIRROR $2.95
                                              Canada $3.50

☐ 51546-3   AS ON A DARKLING PLAIN $3.99
                                              Canada $4.99

☐ 51300-2   BATTLE STATION $3.95
                                              Canada $4.95

☐ 53245-7   COLONY $3.95
                                              Canada $4.95

☐ 50319-8   CYBERBOOKS $4.50
                                              Canada $5.50

☐ 53212-0   ESCAPE PLUS $2.95
                                              Canada $3.50

☐ 53241-4   FUTURE CRIME $4.95
                                              Canada $5.95

☐ 53225-2   MULTIPLE MAN $2.95
                                              Canada $3.95

☐ 51429-7   ORION IN THE DYING TIME $4.99
                                              Canada $5.99

☐ 50238-8   PEACEKEEPERS $4.95
                                              Canada $5.95

Buy them at your local bookstore or use this handy coupon:
Clip and mail this page with your order.

Publishers Book and Audio Mailing Service
P.O. Box 120159, Staten Island, NY 10312-0004

Please send me the book(s) I have checked above. I am enclosing $ _____
(Please add $1.25 for the first book, and $.25 for each additional book to cover postage and handling.
Send check or money order only—no CODs.)

Name _____

Address _____

City _____ State/Zip _____

Please allow six weeks for delivery. Prices subject to change without notice.